# Readers Lo

## *Paint by Number*

"This story, like most of Andrew's books is sweet and full of feelings… If you've never read a book from Andrew Grey and even if you have, I highly recommend this one."
—Open Skye Book Reviews

"There is a saying that you can never go home again but this story will prove an exception to that."
—Paranormal Romance Guild

## *Hard Road Back*

"I urge you to grab a copy of *Hard Road Back* so you too can discover and enjoy Martin and Scarborough's world."
—Love Bytes

## *Catch of a Lifetime*

"…a salute to Mr. Grey's mastery of gay locution, which added enormously to my reading pleasure."
—Rainbow Book Reviews

## *Twice Baked*

"This a great second chance romance novel… There is loads of charm and romance."
—MM Good Book Reviews

"A fun and flirty story I enjoyed and I believe you will, too."
—Bayou Book Junkie

## By ANDREW GREY

Published by DREAMSPINNER PRESS
www.dreamspinnerpress.com

# FIRE AND SAND
# ANDREW GREY

Published by
DREAMSPINNER PRESS

5032 Capital Circle SW, Suite 2, PMB# 279,
Tallahassee, FL 32305-7886  USA
www.dreamspinnerpress.com

This is a work of fiction. Names, characters, places, and incidents either
are the product of author imagination or are used fictitiously, and any
resemblance to actual persons, living or dead, business establishments,
events, or locales is entirely coincidental.

Fire and Sand
© 2022 Andrew Grey.

Cover Art
© 2022 L.C. Chase
http://www.lcchase.com

Cover content is for illustrative purposes only and any person depicted
on the cover is a model.

Mass Market Paperback ISBN: 978-1-64108-299-0
Trade Paperback ISBN: 978-1-64108-298-3
Digital ISBN: 978-1-64108-297-6
Mass Market Paperback published January 2023
v. 1.0

Printed in the United States of America
∞
This paper meets the requirements of
ANSI/NISO Z39.48-1992 (Permanence of Paper).

To Dominic, who always comes to my rescue.

# CHAPTER 1

TROOPER WYATT Nelson sipped his coffee and put the takeout cup in the holder before checking the radar screen again. He had dreamed of being a police officer since he was eight years old. Somehow he hadn't pictured himself sitting beside the highway, watching as cars zipped by, looking for the ones going too fast. Not that he didn't think traffic control was important. Unsafe driving caused accidents and killed people, especially on the curved roads that surrounded Carlisle. The town had lowered the speed limit years ago because of fatal accidents, and drivers still seemed to believe the signs saying to drive fifty-five were only a suggestion. But he had always dreamed of more. He'd seen himself investigating and solving crimes. Troopers needed to pay their dues. After three years, Wyatt hoped that period might be coming to an end for him.

Wyatt shook his head, forcing himself to stay alert and to dispel the state police line he had heard time and time again from his chief. Yeah, the traffic statistics were true enough, but spending the entire day by the side of the highway was about as interesting as watching grass grow. Being a police officer was supposed to be exciting work—

*Yee-ooom…. Yeee-ooom….* Two cars sped by in rapid succession. Wyatt flipped on his lights, turned on the siren, and pulled out. Fortunately, the highway was clear, and he stepped on it as he called in. "Two cars doing eighty-five plus. One chasing the other."

His adrenaline was already pumping as he got up to speed. "Lead car, white late-model Lexus. Chaser, a red Camry, heading south on 81, passing exit forty-four. Request backup." He sped up until he was doing almost ninety-five, but he still didn't make any headway. He could only hope to God that one of them didn't kill themselves or someone else if they lost control.

Dispatch came right back, confirming backup. Wyatt continued driving, the world zipping past his car at an ever-increasing speed. The siren screamed, and other drivers pulled the hell over to get out of the way. Clearing his way through traffic was made easier by the unnerving speed of the other two cars.

The Camry seemed to be losing the race, and Wyatt gained on it and called in the plate to have it run. "Slow your vehicle down and pull over," he said through the speaker, staying behind the losing driver in this two-man race. "Pull over," he repeated.

The Camry finally broke speed, slowed down, and pulled off to the side of the road. Wyatt came to a stop right behind the other car. "Turn off your engine," he said through the speaker and took a deep breath as he waited for the report on the license plate to come back.

His onboard computer flashed the name of the registered owner, Quinton Jackson, age twenty-six, along with a history of traffic and nonviolent offenses dating back to early adulthood. Great, this was going to be interesting. Wyatt didn't know what was going on, and he wasn't taking any chances. He got out of his car, gun and Taser at the ready, and approached the vehicle slowly. The driver's window lowered, and Wyatt waited, ready to take cover if a weapon made an appearance. "Do you have any idea how fast you were going?" Wyatt asked.

"I know. My son is in that car." Instead of the smart-mouthed answer he'd expected, he got near panic. "That's my son's mother's car, and my son is in the back seat. He's three months old, and some asshole stole the car."

In an instant, everything changed. "Let me get this straight—"

"Some guy stole the Lexus, and my son's lunatic mother had left him in the back in his car seat because he was asleep. I'm telling you someone stole the damn car with him in it. For God's sake, do something." Huge blue eyes pleaded with him from inside the car.

Wyatt grabbed his radio. "Possible kidnap victim in back seat of white Lexus. Three-month-old boy in car seat. I repeat, report of a child in the back seat of the white Lexus." *Jesus Christ on the cross.*

"Acknowledged. Car reportedly passing exit thirty-seven, likely heading to Maryland border. All units respond. Issuing Amber Alert." Dispatch was on it, and Wyatt listened to the chatter.

"What's your son's name?"

"Callum Winters, and he's three months old." The disheveled blond man leaned against the steering wheel, his shoulders shaking. "Why would Jennifer just leave him in the damned car? I know that sometimes he can be fussy and hard to get to sleep, but to do that...."

Wyatt made notes on what Mr. Jackson said.

"Troopers have been alerted. In the meantime, let me see your license and registration." He had to know what he was dealing with, and regardless of everything else, he would be expected to do his job thoroughly.

Quinton shakily handed him his license and fished the paperwork out of the glove compartment, the computer printout flapping as he handed it over. "This is the insurance." His voice shook like a leaf in the wind.

"Troopers have closed the highway at mile twenty-two," Dispatch reported, and as Wyatt checked the paperwork, he got an additional report. "White Lexus has been stopped, and child is unharmed and safe." Wyatt sighed as tension eased away. He reported the status of Callum to Quinton, who broke down and cried.

Wyatt returned to his car, ran all of the information he had, and asked for guidance on any citation to be given. He knew what had happened and what Quinton had done, but giving the guy a ticket, especially one for that speed—after he was just trying to protect his son—seemed like adding insult to injury.

Once he had his answer, he returned to Quinton's car and handed him his license and paperwork. "By all rights, I should give you one hell of a speeding ticket and possibly take you in for reckless endangerment. But given the circumstances, I'm going to let you off with a warning."

"What about Callum? Where is he?"

"Troopers have him in custody, and Child Services has been called. It's standard procedure in a case like this. They need to investigate with the mother why Callum was left unattended in a car."

Quinton groaned, seeming wrung out. "I know you're only doing what you have to do, but he has to have been scared enough as it was, and now for strangers to be with him…."

"They're still at the scene up ahead. Like I said, Child Services will be called, but if you follow me, I'll lead you up to where your son is." Wyatt returned to his car and pulled out when it was safe for both of them to enter the highway. He kept an eye on the car behind him as they stayed with the flow of traffic. Once it slowed as they approached where the Lexus sat on the side of the road, Wyatt moved out of the lane and traveled down the shoulder to where the other troopers had gathered. He parked and directed Quinton to do the same.

"That's my son," Quinton said as he hurried to where Louise Graves, one of Wyatt's fellow troopers, held the child carrier. He had his son out of the carrier and in his arms in seconds.

"We have a number of questions for you," Louise said sternly. It was her way.

Quinton immediately went on defense. "Callum's mother left him alone in the back of the car because he was sleeping. I was on my way to pick him up when I saw a man"—he held his son closer, tears in his eyes—"get in the car and take off with it. I chased him to try to get my son back." He was nearly frantic once again and turned away from all of them, rocking his child slowly to try to soothe the now crying baby. "There should be a diaper bag somewhere, I hope. Maybe in the trunk of the car."

"We've been trying to get in touch with the child's mother," Louise gruffed. "Is she your wife?"

Quinton shook his head. "God, no. She was my one-time mistake. I tried it with a woman one time, and we had Callum." He smiled down at the squirming bundle in his arms. "Jennifer isn't particularly motherly. I think her parents put a lot of pressure on her to keep Callum." He smiled as he held his son's hand. It looked to Wyatt like Quinton had a real bond with him. "I wanted to take him, but I don't know if I'm a much better parent." He met Wyatt's gaze with such intensity in his blue eyes that it immediately got under Wyatt's professional façade. "I haven't exactly been a saint myself."

"Donald from Child Services is on his way. It's a weekend, but I had his number, and he said he'd be here as soon as possible," Louise reported. Wyatt knew that the gruffness and cold professionalism were just acts she used to cover up the fact that she was a huge bowl of mush on the inside, especially when children were involved. She and her partner had two kids and were apparently considering having a third.

Wyatt half expected a fight from Quinton. "Good. Something has to change. Callum deserves better." He still held his son, and Wyatt started to wonder.

"Has there been any word from the mother?" Wyatt asked Louise.

"No. Officers have been sent to the house, but no one was home." She drew closer. "What the hell kind of mother leaves a little baby like that and goes off to whatever the hell else she thinks she has to do?" Anger flared in her eyes for only a second, and then her badass persona slipped back into place.

"At least the father is here," Wyatt commented.

She met his gaze, and Wyatt knew what she was thinking. This guy's record was unlikely to put him up for Father of the Year.

"He did go after his son and tried to get him back." Wyatt could only imagine the level of panic any parent would feel if their child had been taken the way Callum had. "What would you do if it had been one of your kids?"

Louise took a split second. "I'd make sure they never found the damned body." He'd expected no less from her.

A car pulled up behind the others along the side of the road as a tow truck came to haul away the Lexus. Traffic was flowing well on the freeway now. A man got out of the car and approached them, smiling at Louise. "Donald Ickle," he said to Wyatt. "I'm the Child Services supervisor for the county."

Wyatt took the lead, explaining what happened, at least as far as they knew. Then Quinton took over, telling them what he found when he'd gone to pick up Callum. He answered all their questions, holding Callum to him. "Is there someplace other than the side of the highway that we can go? I need to get him fed and cared for."

"I found this in the trunk of the car before it was towed." Louise handed Callum a diaper bag.

"I agree. What I'm going to propose is that we head back into Carlisle."

"I need to get Callum home," Quinton said. "I'll give you my address, and if you want to come there, you're welcome to. I'll answer any questions you have." The scene around them was clearing.

"Is that okay with you?" Donald asked Wyatt, and he nodded. "Then we'll meet at Quinton's house in half an hour." He turned to Quinton. "As a word of warning, I have every right to remove Callum from your custody and place him in emergency protection. Don't make me use it." Wyatt figured Quinton was getting the "ice-Ickle" treatment that Donald was famous for. Wyatt suspected he'd be cold too, with the things Donald saw every single day.

"I won't," Quinton said firmly. "I want what's best for Callum." He placed his son back in his car seat and carried him to the Camry. Wyatt went along, verified that the baby was secured properly, and then let Quinton enter the flow of traffic. He followed on the freeway. They turned around to head back north and then got off at Hanover Street and headed toward town. Quinton pulled up in front of a tiny row house on the north side of town. Wyatt parked behind him and got out as another car pulled to a stop just up the block. A woman about Quinton's age in yoga pants and a top at least one size too big got out of the passenger side and charged up to Quinton. She looked ferocious with her hair all askew, lips drawn into a line. The car pulled away, and Wyatt noticed the lighted Lyft sign in the window.

"What the hell do you think you're doing? Where's my car? What did you do with it?" She reached for the baby carrier.

"Stop, ma'am," Wyatt said.

"What's going on and what's he done now?" she demanded. "I want my baby back. I'm going to report you to Child Services and make sure you never see Callum again." Her eyes blazed.

"Jennifer, Child Services will be here in fifteen minutes or so." Quinton unlocked the door and went inside. She went to follow, but he barred the way. "You need to stay outside."

"What? Where's my car? What did you do with it?"

"Are you Jennifer Winters?" Wyatt asked.

"Yes. What of it?"

Wyatt wondered how Quinton could have possibly picked this harpy to experiment with. "Your car was stolen, and since you left your baby in the back seat, he was taken along with the car. Callum is okay, but Mr. Jackson was trying to get him back." She gave him a cold stare, but that was nothing, and Wyatt waited her out. "What was your son doing in the car unattended?"

"He'd finally gone to sleep, and I didn't want to wake him. My neighbor picked up some things at the store for me, and we got to talking. I was just next door." She made it sound like it wasn't a big deal. "I knew Quint was coming over to pick him up, so...." She shrugged.

"You figured you'd leave the baby alone." Now it was his turn to glare. "And the result is that your car was stolen and your child abducted." The smugness in her expression began to fade. God, this person was a real piece of work.

Donald pulled up, and Wyatt took charge, explaining what he'd discovered and what he'd already been told. He had enough evidence for a child endangerment charge and requested another vehicle as backup. He had the idea that as soon as he told Jennifer exactly what was going to happen, she would realize this was going to be a lot more than just an inconvenience—and become a much bigger problem to deal with. "I want to see Callum. He's my child, and I have a right to see that he's okay," Jennifer demanded.

"Quinton is Callum's biological father?" Donald asked.

"Yes, and I have the paternity test to prove it. Why? Is the swisher trying to claim that he isn't the father? I have proof, no matter what he says about not liking women." She sneered.

Wyatt wanted to step in to say that talking that way to another gay man was not going to get her anywhere. "That's enough. We were only verifying Callum's paternity. Donald, go on inside and take care of what you need to. I'll stay out here with the mother until you're done." He stepped back, and Donald went inside.

"I know my rights, and you can't keep me away from my child. I want to see Callum, and he's coming home with me. I have custody of him from the court, and you can't override that." She put her hands on her hips as though she knew she was right.

"Ma'am, I need you to calm down and just relax. A report has been made, and it must be investigated. That's the law. You need to be patient." He crossed his arms over his chest and stayed between her and the door in case she tried to bust inside.

A car from the local police arrived, as did a second trooper. "Hey, Wyatt," Kip Rogers said as he got out of his patrol car. "I heard you were handling something here in town. Just thought I'd see if I could assist." Kip was an amazing officer Wyatt had gotten to know since his patrol area included Carlisle.

"Thanks. I appreciate that." He stepped to the side and spoke softly with Kip about what he expected to take place. "She's going to fight like a banshee when she realizes what's going to happen."

Donald called Wyatt inside, and Kip agreed to stay with Jennifer. "Everything is good here. The home is clean, and he has supplies and a proper place for Callum to stay. He is the natural father, so placing Callum here is no issue."

"Thanks. I'll leave you to it." He stepped outside and faced Jennifer.

"What's happening? I want my child. You can't just take him from me."

"Jennifer Winters, you are being charged with child endangerment for leaving Callum in the car. I'm placing you under arrest." He read her her rights, and she came unglued.

Wyatt cuffed her as a stream of screamed obscenities bounced off the fronts of the homes across the street. Wyatt felt sorry for them, but he got Jennifer into the car and closed the door to cut off her yelling.

Donald and Quinton came outside, and Quinton had Callum in his arms.

"If there's anything we can do to help, just let either myself or Donald know," Wyatt said. He gave him a card and got into the car, grateful that Jennifer had decided the stop her yelling. Hopefully Callum would be in a good home and well taken care of by his father. Wyatt's last thought was that it was a shame that he was unlikely to ever see Quinton again. For some reason that made him sad... until Jennifer began cursing him out and distracted him once again.

# CHAPTER 2

QUINTON LET the old, drab curtains fall back into place as Jennifer was put in the back of a police car. Why in the hell had he decided that sleeping with her would be a good idea? Heck, he was gay, and sure, he liked women, but not to sleep with. Well, he did get one good thing out of it, and that was the amazing bundle of warmth curled against him. Quinton rocked gently back and forth as he tried to soothe Callum into a deeper sleep.

He had made some bad decisions in his life, and getting involved with her was only the latest in a string of them. If there was something stupid to be done, chances were Quinton had done it at one time or another. It would be easy for him to blame it on his mother. His father had never been in the picture, and his mother had never been a paragon of virtue. She liked her men, and there had been a parade of them through their lives over the years. As he got older, Quinton figured he needed to make his own way, and he'd done that by taking whatever he needed. If that meant food from the grocery store or some cash grabbed out of a register while the clerk wasn't looking, so be it. The other kids in school had decent clothes that weren't falling apart at the seams, so why shouldn't he?

A knock at the door pulled him out of his thoughts, and he opened it. Donald stood there, and Quinton let him back inside. "Jennifer is being taken into custody."

Quinton nodded. He figured that. "What happens next?"

"Well, she'll be arraigned, and she might be offered bail. If she gets out...."

"Will she get Callum back?" He held his son closer, rubbing his back lightly as he slept. Callum always slept well for him, and all it had taken was that first look into his son's blue eyes for him to fall in love.

"It's unlikely, given the nature of the charges." Donald glanced around, and Quinton offered him a seat on his thrift-store sofa. Donald had already proven to be a straight shooter. Quinton liked that. At least he knew where he stood. "However, the courts will make the determination."

"I want to keep my son. I wanted to get custody before but was told because of his age and the fact that I have a record and stuff that it was very unlikely." He slowly sat down so he didn't disturb Callum.

"Yes. That's very true. On paper you seem like you'd make a marginal parent, and I have to be honest, I'm inclined to put Callum in emergency foster care just as a precaution. Like I said, on paper you aren't a good risk." He sat back and continued to watch him. "But it's also apparent that you love Callum and have his best interests at heart. And the trooper who helped rescue Callum spoke on your behalf. He told me how frantic you were to get Callum back and how distraught and upset you were about him being taken. You apparently went to great lengths and took risks to yourself to try to save him." Donald's gaze turned cold. "I trust you don't intend to repeat that kind of risky behavior with Callum?"

There was another knock at the door, and Quinton shook his head before getting up from the mismatched chair. He opened the door and was surprised to see the hot and hunky state trooper on his doorstep. He couldn't remember his name. Hell, after realizing Callum had been taken, he couldn't remember a lot other than his need to try to save him. "I…." He peered outside. "I thought you took Jennifer into custody?"

"The local police department claimed jurisdiction, so she was transferred to their car, and they will book her. Since the initial crime took place here in town with her leaving the child in the car, they are more than willing to move forward with the prosecution." He seemed relieved. "I'm on my way back out on patrol, but I wanted to make sure that Callum was all right."

"What about the car thief?" Quinton asked.

"He's in custody as well." Trooper Hunky watched both of them, and for a second, Quinton wondered just what the broad-shouldered man looked like without that uniform on. Jesus, he was not going to have those kinds of thoughts about a cop. "What's next?"

Donald sighed. "I'm trying to determine placement for Callum until there's a hearing."

"I see," Trooper Hunky said. Quinton needed to stop thinking of him that way. His badge said Nelson, and he needed to remember that. "Mr. Jackson is Callum's biological father." A light of hope seemed to brighten the room for Quinton.

"Yes." Donald stood. "I'm inclined to leave Callum in his care until permanent placement can be sorted out."

Quinton sighed and left the room. He put Callum in his new white crib in the corner of his bedroom and grabbed a towel to wipe his eyes. Shit, he didn't cry. At least he hadn't in years. Not even when the police had tried to scare the hell out of him the last time he'd been taken into custody just before he'd turned eighteen. The boy he'd been arrested for shoplifting with had wept like a girl, but not him. Quinton had determined a long time ago that showing weakness was the easiest way to get hurt. Bury your emotions and come out fighting. It was better to go down that way than in a pool of weakness. Still, at this moment, the thought of losing Callum when he had the chance to do right by his son was too much to take.

"Mr. Jackson?" Trooper Hunky said from outside the door.

He gave his face another wipe and blinked before leaving the room. "I needed to get Callum down. I'm sorry."

"Donald will stop by occasionally to check on Callum, and he's asked if I would be willing to as well as a favor. I'll be honest, we both have... concerns because of your past, but we are in agreement that as his father, you are the person best to build a relationship with him."

"You have our cards. Call us if you have any questions." Donald walked toward the door. "What hours do you work?"

"They vary. I work maintenance at Dickinson College. Mostly I work normal hours during the day." Shit, he was going to need to arrange for day care. Jennifer had something set up for Callum, but she had refused to put Wyatt on the list of people to pick him up or drop him off.

"Okay. I have a contact at the college's day care, and I'll arrange for a voucher and for Callum to be enrolled. Give me a few hours and I'll call you with the details." Donald paused. "Parenting is a huge job. I want to set you up with some classes that we're running that could help you with some of the skills you're going to need."

Quinton nodded as the overwhelming level of the task ahead bore down on him. "I want Callum to have a better childhood and more of a chance in life than I did. You tell me where I need to be and I'll be there." He hoped he sounded as determined as he felt.

"That's good." Donald said goodbye and left, along with Trooper Hunky… Nelson.

Quinton locked the door and checked on his still-sleeping son before going to the kitchen. He finally had a chance to go through the diaper bag and could only shake his head. He found one bottle with formula powder in it ready to be made up, a few diapers, and a change of clothes. That was all he had to start with. Quinton also checked where he kept his own baby supplies. Fortunately, he had a case of diapers and some formula that he'd gotten the last time Callum had stayed with him. He had a few onesies and some other clothes, but nowhere near enough if Callum was going to come home with him to live.

He made himself a light dinner, his stomach still riled after all the excitement. After a few bites of his bologna sandwich, he set it down, wondering what he had gotten himself into. He wasn't equipped to raise a child. Hell, what did he know about babies? His experience was through his own mother, and Lord knows that wasn't going to help with shit. There was no one he could call for help. His mother lived on the other side of town, but going to her was a last resort. No, he was on his own, and somehow Quinton was going to have to pull his life together, figure shit out, and make things the very best he could for Callum. That was all there was to it.

TWO EVENINGS later, Quinton sat in a classroom at the high school with Callum asleep in his carrier. With

Donald's help, Quinton had made it through the ensuing couple of days. Donald had stopped by and delivered some vouchers to help with supplies, and he'd even gotten some clothes for Callum. At least some of his worries could recede for a little while. Now Quinton hoped to learn how to be a better parent.

"Being a parent is the most important and hardest job most of us ever have," said Wendy, the leader of the class, after introducing herself. "I have two boys and a little girl of my own, and raising them to be productive, self-assured people is the toughest thing I have ever done, and I'm trained in child development."

The door to the class opened, and Quinton was shocked when in walked Trooper Hunky—umm, Nelson—in civilian clothes. Somehow he looked even better than in his uniform.

Quinton wondered if he was here to help teach the class, but he took a seat at the desk next to Wyatt's and shared a smile. The instructor continued, and Quinton forced himself to pay attention to her rather than constantly glancing at the person next to him. He needed to be real. Quinton had a son that he was responsible for. A romance with someone was not in the cards. Chasing after guys and trying to get laid had led him into trouble in the past, and he needed to keep his head where it belonged—on being the best parent he could be for Callum. His mother had spent years chasing after guys, always hoping the next one she met was going to be the good one who would make her life better. All they did was make her life worse. He wasn't going to do that to Callum. And it didn't matter if the guy was a super hot police officer.

He forced his attention on the class and took notes, even raising his hand to ask a question at one point.

That was something he had avoided doing his entire
tenure in high school. He was pretty proud of himself.
Just about the time the instructor called for a break,
Callum woke. Quinton got him changed, fed, and then
joined the others for a cup of coffee.

"He seems pretty happy."

"I like to think he is, Trooper," Quinton said as he
carefully sipped from the foam cup, sitting in a folding
chair with Callum in his carrier on the floor in front of
him.

"Call me Wyatt, please." He smiled down at Callum, took the next seat, and offered his finger. Callum
latched right on, smiling a little, his eyes bright.

"What are you doing here? Do you have kids too?"
Quinton asked. It seemed like a stupid question. Even
if he did, why would a police officer need to take parenting classes?

"I'm a registered foster parent. I usually take children in for short-term stays while the courts are trying
to make a decision or for emergency placement. I have
to maintain that certification, and I needed a class to do
it. This one fit my schedule." He sipped his coffee. "I'm
glad to see that you're here and that Callum is doing
so well."

"The initial hearing is in a few weeks, and I want
to make sure I've done everything I can." It was going
to be tough, working all day, going to classes, taking
care of Callum, and just moving forward with their
lives, but he was going to make it happen, one way or
another. "I understand that Jennifer is still in jail."

Wyatt nodded. "I've been told they expect her to
make bail soon. At this point, she isn't supposed to
see Callum on her own, and any visitations need to
be worked out through Child Services. They'll have

someone there to supervise them. So if she stops by the house, tell her to leave, and if she refuses, call the police for backup." He was so intense, like he was still on the job.

"Do you ever really relax?" Quinton asked. "It's like you're a plainclothes trooper." He had to smile, because in any clothes, Wyatt was something else. His shirt was tight enough to accentuate his arms, and it pulled across his chest just right. Quinton looked away so he didn't blush or seem too interested. He had no idea how Wyatt would react to interest from another guy.

"I suppose I tend to be on a lot of the time." He sipped some more coffee and smiled. "Now, this little guy." He played footsy with Callum, who seemed fascinated with Wyatt. Quinton lifted Callum out of the seat, and he went right into Wyatt's arms. "Hey, big boy, are you being good for Daddy?"

Callum blew bubbles as he held Wyatt's finger. "He's been really happy. Jennifer always said that she could never get him to go to sleep and that he was fussy and irritable all the time."

"Have you seen that?" Wyatt didn't look away from Callum. "He seems like a perfectly happy baby to me."

Quinton took Callum and rocked him slightly, hoping he would go back to sleep. Fortunately, when he placed him back in the carrier, Callum closed his eyes, and that seemed to be it. "How long is he sleeping at night?"

Quinton tried not to sigh. "About three hours. I honestly don't know how parents do it. I got up this morning and almost brushed my teeth with diaper cream. At lunch, I eat and put my head down for a twenty-minute nap because I'm so tired."

"Welcome to parenthood," the instructor said as she pulled a chair to sit in front of him. "The best advice I can give you is to learn to sleep when you can. If your little one is sleeping, try to nap yourself." She leaned closer. "And if you have vacation time from work, take a day here and there, still take Callum to day care, and just rest for a while."

"And don't be afraid to ask for help," Wyatt added.

"Amen to that," Wendy said.

Quinton nodded. He liked the idea about vacation. He had some time built up, so maybe he could use it get some things done.

"Especially your family," Wyatt said.

"I really don't have much of one. My sister lives in North Carolina with her girlfriend, and my mother…." He did sigh this time. "My mother and I don't get along. About four years ago she found Jesus, and that meant that her gay son didn't exactly fit in her life. Then that same son tried to fit in and got someone pregnant." He glanced at Callum. "It's just him and me for as long as I get to have him." The thought of Callum being taken away sent a chill up his spine that he couldn't stop, no matter how much he might want to. Quinton was well aware that it was likely he would have to return Callum to his mother. "Sorry. I didn't mean to give an entire dysfunctional family history."

"What about close friends?" Wendy asked. "People you trust."

Quinton swallowed and shook his head. "Let's just say that I'm a product of my family and that I made plenty of mistakes. I'm trying not to repeat them." It sounded stupid. There were so many things in his life that didn't fit in with Callum and what he needed.

"I see," Wendy said. "A lot of the parents here are facing the same challenges. You aren't alone." She smiled and stood, then moved on to another group of students. Quinton finished his coffee and tried not to think too much about what was ahead.

"My advice is to try to take things one day at a time," Wyatt said. "I know it sounds trite and all, but it's true. Think about today and maybe tomorrow. Baby steps are about all that most of us can handle." Quinton got another smile, and Wendy called the class back to order.

Quinton took notes and listened; Callum slept. It was a good class, and once it was over, Quinton felt as though he had some things he could use to make his and Callum's life better. "Have you had dinner?" Wyatt asked as class broke up and Quinton gently lifted Callum's carrier.

"Not yet."

"Would you like to get something to eat? I know a nice Italian place. The food is good." Wyatt seemed a little nervous.

Quinton glanced down at Callum just as his stomach rumbled. He made a quick mental check of his budget and figured that as long as he was careful, he could have dinner out. "Sounds good." For a quick second he wondered if Wyatt was asking him out on a date, but that was probably silly. He pushed the notion aside, even as a zing of excitement he couldn't ignore raced up his back, like he was at the beginning of something special. But Quinton needed to go slow and be wary. He didn't usually have much luck... with just about anything.

# CHAPTER 3

"MAN, THE portions here are huge," Quinton said as he set his dish of pasta aside. "Will they bring a container?"

Wyatt smiled. Quinton had hummed over his pasta the entire meal. The sounds were almost as enticing as the food. "Sure they will." He leaned over to where Callum was yawning. He opened his blue eyes, blinking, and then screwed up his face like he was getting ready to squawk. "Can I feed him?"

Quinton got out a bottle from the diaper bag, then filled it with warm water from a Thermos, and Wyatt lifted Callum out of the carrier, set him across his legs, and supported Callum's head and back while giving him the bottle. The little guy sucked for all he was worth. "He must have been hungry."

"Callum is always hungry. When he wakes up, he wants a bottle *right now*." Quinton drank some of his soda. He'd been a little jumpy through dinner.

"The two of you are getting along well?" Wyatt asked. It sure seemed to him like they were. Callum seemed bright-eyed, well fed, and happy.

"Yes." Quinton set down his red plastic soda cup.

Wyatt smiled down at Callum. "You have nothing to be nervous about." He kept his attention on Callum. "I'm not looking to haul you into jail or something."

"Sorry. It's… well…," Quinton stammered. "You already know my legal history from the other day, I'm sure. It's not like I'm squeaky clean. And the only times

I've been around police officers were when I was in trouble." He smiled, but the nerves were still there. "It's nice that you asked me to have dinner with you and all, but what would a state police trooper want with a loser like me?" Quinton looked down at the table, picking at a piece of pasta with his fork before eating it. "The other day when you stopped me on the freeway, I was so panicked. I expected you to take me in. I didn't think you were going to believe me about the carjacking and Callum, but you did." He lifted his gaze, and damn, Wyatt had expressive eyes.

"I'm not a dick, and while it's my job to enforce the law, part of that is to keep people safe. Callum was in danger, and I'm glad the little guy was unhurt." He gently patted his back, and Callum burped like a sailor. Wyatt chuckled as he gave him the bottle once more. He'd asked himself a few times during dinner what he saw in Quinton and even why he had extended the invitation in the first place. Maybe he was just a softie at heart, but everyone deserved a chance, and maybe giving one to Quinton was also giving Callum a chance at the same time. After all, if Quinton could build a good life for himself, then Callum would have a chance to grow up in a healthy environment. Quinton had already said that his family was dysfunctional, and children of those type of families often created the same type of family.

"So am I some kind of social experiment?"

"No." Wyatt swallowed a chuckle. He didn't think Quinton would appreciate it. "You're obviously trying." He leaned over the table. "There were twenty parents in that class tonight, and more than half of them have taken it before and were ordered by the court to be there last night. Some were on their phones, probably playing Candy Crush. You, on the other hand, asked questions and even took notes. You really wanted to learn something."

"I'm really trying to do what's right for Callum. He doesn't need four different men in his life that he's called Daddy at one point or other."

Wyatt did a double take. "Did that happen to you?"

Quinton nodded. "My mother dates guys until she gets tired of them. Sometimes it takes a year or two, but then she finds out they aren't going to be able to give her what she really wants, which is a life of leisure. So she dumps them and goes looking for someone else. I had four men would-be dads by the time I was ten. After that, I just lost track and did my best to stay away. A few of them really tried to get to know me and to build a relationship. The best one was Charlie. He still lives in town, and I see him every now and then. He's a really good person, though I always wondered what he ever saw in my mother."

"What does he think about Callum?" Wyatt asked.

"I told him about him the last time I saw him, and Charlie hugged me and told me that he was thrilled to be a grandpa." Quinton's voice broke, and Wyatt pretended not to hear it. "I wish he had been my biological father. At least then maybe I would have had some kind of chance."

Callum finished his bottle, and Wyatt burped him again and then handed him over to Quinton so he could be changed.

While he was in the restroom, Wyatt took care of the check and asked the server to box up the rest of the food. He also asked for drink refills. When Quinton returned, he placed Callum in his carrier, and the baby closed his eyes and seemed to fall asleep. "What's your family like?"

Wyatt almost couldn't believe he was going to talk about his history, but if Quinton could, then he would share as well. "My parents died when I was five, so I was placed in foster care. That's why I do what I do with other kids. I was adopted by a really nice family from Shippensburg when I was thirteen. They were my foster parents before that. I was really lucky. They already had a son of their own, Randy, and he became my older brother. Today he's a Marine Corps captain. My parents are proud of both of us. I was very lucky. My adoptive family never treated me any differently than they did Randy."

Quinton sipped his soda. "My sister has done well. She worked and paid her way through college, probably on sheer will and determination. After her sophomore year, she rarely came home at all. I think she liked college and being away from the chaos of our mother, so she just stayed away." He shrugged. "I missed her so much. She was like my ally, and she helped make parts of my life normal. After she was gone, I started getting into trouble more and more. I know I disappointed Nancy a lot, but she wasn't here."

"Does she know about Callum?" Wyatt asked, curious.

Quinton smiled and nodded. "She was the one who sent me the crib and the baby furniture—all of it. This afternoon there was a knock on the door, and it was the Amazon truck delivering two cases of diapers, formula, and even some clothes, as well as a stuffed rabbit for Callum." His voice hitched. "I really wish she and Margie were here in town. I know I could rely on them. Nancy and Margie have been trying to have a baby of their own, but they aren't having any luck."

Wyatt wrapped his hands around his cool drink glass, but he wasn't interested in the contents. He found himself getting lost in Quinton's eyes and had to keep himself from drifting off into some fanciful ridiculousness. "What did she think about you and Jennifer?"

"Oh God," Quinton said. "She asked me if I was crazy and why I would ever get involved with an absolute nutcase like her. Nancy knew her from school and thought her selfish and foolish. I guess I probably should have listened to Nancy and stayed away. It would have saved me a great deal of crazy drama. But then I wouldn't have Callum, and I'll take having him in my life, no matter the price." The small smile that tugged at Quinton's lips shone with pure love.

Callum stretched and began kicking. "Do you need to get him home?" Wyatt asked. He normally didn't talk about things like this, and if they stayed here any longer, he might start telling Quinton his deepest and darkest secrets. Wyatt couldn't remember the last time he'd talked this much about himself.

"I really should. He's been so good for the entire class and now dinner that I'm afraid it's about to come to an end and Mr. Fussypants is about to make an appearance. Thank you for everything." He seemed to be looking for the check, and Wyatt explained that it was all set. He was surprised and thanked Wyatt for dinner.

"I'll see you in class on Thursday," Wyatt said, motioning for Quinton to go first. Wyatt followed him out, and they went to their cars. Wyatt drove home but couldn't stop thinking about Quinton. He wished he could figure out what it was about him that piqued his interest and got around the barriers he'd set up long ago to protect himself.

"HEY, MOM." Wyatt answered his phone as he closed the front door behind him. When he had been accepted onto the force a few years earlier, he'd started saving, and last year he'd purchased a small home on a quiet street just south of downtown.

"Busy day?"

"I was in class and then went out with one of the parents." He placed his keys in the bowl near the door and checked that the door was locked before he went through to the living room. The house was fairly open, which gave the illusion of space. "I told you about the little one who was in the back of a car when it was stolen. Well, this was the father."

She clicked her tongue. "How can people be so careless?"

"I wish it was only that. Anyway, the father seems to be taking things seriously." Once he'd gotten off shift, he had called his mother. While he'd been on duty, he'd been fine. But only his mother knew how upset the entire incident had made him. Cases involving children always unsettled him.

"That's a good thing for the father and for his son." She sounded a little off.

"Is something going on?" he asked.

His mother sighed and hesitated. That meant there was something she was trying to work up to saying. "Your father is going into the hospital for some tests. He's been having stomach issues, and they want to see what's happening. The gastroenterologist is afraid that it's an ulcer. If it is, they want to determine how serious it is."

"When? I'll arrange for time off so I can sit with you."

"No. He's going in have the tests tomorrow. If they need to operate, I'll call you and you can take some time off, but not until then. I already called your brother, but he isn't able to get leave right now. He didn't say anything, but I'm guessing that they're gearing up for a deployment of some kind." She was always able to read between the military lines to know what was going on. Sometimes Wyatt swore the NSA should give his mother a job as a code breaker, because she could divine more information from a single clue than any person on the planet.

"Okay." He sat in his favorite chair, putting his feet up on the matching ottoman. "Just let me know and I'll make the arrangements."

"Good. Now tell me about this young man you had dinner with," she pressed. "Is he nice? Was this a date-type dinner, or just a going-out-after-class dinner that might turn into a date later?" Sometimes his mother could be voracious. She was intent on marrying her boys off. So far neither of them had taken the bait. Well, Randy dated some, but he hadn't found the right girl yet, though according to him, he kept trying.

"Mom, it was just dinner after class." He tried to keep any sort of annoyance out of his voice, but he must have failed.

"Are you sure about that?" Wyatt groaned, and of course she picked up on that. "You like this guy."

"Jesus, Mother. Stop with the mama superpowers, okay? It was just dinner after class. You know, I'm thinking you should get yourself a hobby. Maybe the

CIA could use you to extract information from prisoners. Put that talent to good use." He rolled his eyes, knowing she couldn't see. At least he hoped not. Lord knows, when he was growing up, she'd always had eyes in the back of her head. Maybe now she'd developed roving ones that had taken up residency in his house.

"I just want you to find someone. You've been alone too long, and the last person you dated...." The ice in her voice said plenty. She had hated Ned on sight. Not that he was the greatest guy on earth, but Mom had hated the man instantly. Still, she had done her best to get along with him for the six months he and Ned dated, and once it was over, Wyatt had been thankful she hadn't baked a cake and thrown a party. "So what's this young man like? I know he has a baby and all. But what else?"

"He's nice, and he's had a hard life, but he's trying to turn himself around for the sake of his child. His family life is pretty much nonexistent, and he doesn't have any support from those few he does have. Though I think that's because he doesn't trust them. I don't know. I haven't met them, but he's trying to take care of his son pretty much alone. And there's a lot of uncertainty there as far as the mother is concerned." He paused. "I sort of arrested her the other day."

"I think you told me," she said.

"Yeah. Well, it's complicated." To top it off, Quinton had a very complicated legal past that had Wyatt worried. He believed Quinton when he said he was trying to do what was right for Callum, but he was well aware of how hard it was for someone to change.

"Life is always complicated, sweetheart. There's very little that's simple and straightforward." Wyatt knew that was true. "But it sounds like this guy has captured your interest. You be careful, but don't close yourself off." She knew him so danged well. "And when you're ready, you bring him home for the mama smell test. I'll know if he's right for you or not." She said good night. "I love you, sweetheart."

She ended the call, and Wyatt set his phone aside with a sigh. Sometimes she was scary, but in a good way.

Wyatt picked up the remote and turned on the television. He found an old movie and settled in to watch the antics of a cat who inherited a baseball team.

God, Wyatt had always expected his life would be much more exciting than this once he joined the force. On television, the state police were always chasing criminals down the highway, busting up drug rings, or rescuing kidnap victims. Well, in the past week, he'd done a couple of those things. Mostly his job was a whole lot of waiting, watching, and patrolling for a little activity and excitement. He loved his job, that was a definite, but Wyatt also wanted more in his life.

He had always found it difficult to make friends. Even on the force, it wasn't easy. Being a trooper meant that going to work was getting in the car and heading out to his duty territory. He didn't spend time in the state police offices drinking coffee and waiting for something to happen. Wyatt was out on patrol. More than once he'd found himself on one side of his territory when a call came in for the other side. And he didn't just patrol the highways. For more than half the state, the state police were the only law enforcement. Wyatt truly loved his work, but that wasn't to say that it didn't have its challenges.

Maybe he should just go to bed and put all his lonely thoughts to sleep. He really had a good life. He could complain all he wanted, but guys like Quinton had it a lot harder than he did.

Wyatt shook his head, wondering why he couldn't get Quinton out of it. Ever since that highway stop, his mind kept going to him. Wyatt had been surprised when he'd walked into class and seen Quinton in one of the chairs with Callum asleep in his carrier next to him. He definitely hadn't been expecting it, nor could he stop the smile. What he really needed to do was to find someone to spend some time with. The hours he spent alone were starting to get to him. Yeah, he probably shouldn't think this way, but it was hard. Quinton had a very troubled past with the law, so maybe it wouldn't be a good idea for them to be anything other than casual acquaintances. But damn, those intense blue eyes drew him in, and Quinton seemed so earnest in how he wanted to make things better for himself and Callum.

Wyatt turned off the television because he wasn't really watching the movie anyhow, and went upstairs. He got undressed and brushed his teeth before slipping under the blankets and picking up the Clive Cussler Dirk Pitt adventure book from the nightstand. Maybe reading would take his mind off Quinton. Nothing else seemed to, so maybe a good book and a case of exhaustion would be able to calm his mind and work their wonders. At least he could try.

# CHAPTER 4

"So now you're awake and want to play," Quinton said to Callum once he got him home from day care the following day. Work had been off the charts, requiring a number of emergency fixes to one of the dorm water systems. Fortunately, he had the experience needed and was able to fix the pipes before they flooded the building's basement.

He took Callum out of his carrier and placed him on a blanket on the floor. Then he set up an activity set that had arrived from Nancy just yesterday. Callum batted the animals with his hands and kicked his feet, having a baby good time.

Quinton took a few minutes to write his sister a thank-you note and send her a picture of Callum as he played.

A hard knock on the front door made him jump. Callum started as well and began to fuss. Quinton picked him up to soothe him as the pounding repeated. He went to the door and peered out the small window. "I know you're in there, and I want to see my baby," Jennifer demanded through the door.

"You can't be here," Quinton told her. "And I can't let you see him. That's what Child Services said. Go home and you can arrange a visit."

She set her jaw and then began swearing at him loud enough for the neighborhood to hear.

He grabbed Wyatt's card and called the number on it. It surprised him when Wyatt picked up right away.

"Jennifer is here at the house. She's pounding on the door, demanding to see Callum." She beat the door again, loudly enough that Wyatt was certain to hear it through the phone.

"I'm on my way back to town from my shift. Let me get you some backup. Don't let her in. Help is on the way." He hung up, and Quinton tried again to reason with Jennifer.

"You need to go through Child Services. They placed Callum here and—"

The pop of what sounded like gunfire rang through the house. Quinton hurried away from the door and went deeper into the house, with Callum screaming. Shit, she'd really gone off the deep end. Jennifer was still screaming as sirens drew closer to the house. His phone rang, and he snatched it out of his pocket.

"I'm out front with two local police. They're getting Jennifer calmed down and have her away from the door."

"I think she took a shot at us. Be careful." His insides felt queasy, and he held Callum, trying to comfort him while controlling the rising panic that she might have hurt Callum.

"She's under control," Wyatt promised.

Quinton approached the front door and peered outside before unlocking it.

Wyatt stepped around what appeared to be shards of the remnants of Quinton's storm door. "Are you and Callum all right?" Wyatt asked immediately.

Quinton nodded, rocking slowly as Callum calmed a little.

"I want to see my baby!" Jennifer demanded. Two uniformed police officers stood blocking her path forward. One of them was the same officer from earlier.

Quinton thought he remembered Wyatt calling him Kip. His badge read Rogers.

"Ma'am, that isn't possible," Wyatt told her calmly. "Your visitation will be supervised, and you aren't to bother Mr. Jackson. This isn't something in his control either." Jennifer's eyes seemed like they were on fire. If this had been a Hollywood horror movie, they would be glowing, and horns would sprout from her forehead.

Quinton shook his head. "Thank you for coming," he told the police officers and turned to what was left of his door. "Did you kick it?"

Jennifer nodded.

"Please make note of that. She damaged property in her attempt to get inside the house." Quinton turned Callum away from her, shielding him with his body.

"Don't you dare!" Jennifer ground between her teeth. "You butt-fucker. So help me, I'll make you pay for this." She struggled as the officers tried to calm her down.

"I need to get Callum inside and away from this. You do what you need to do." To a degree, Quinton was aware he was playing to the audience.

"Do you want to return to jail?" one of the officers asked Jennifer, and she calmed down fast. Then the officer turned to Quinton. "What would you like us to do with her? She has damaged property."

"I'll turn it in to the landlord, and he can decide what he wants to do. I don't own the house." That was the most he could do since she hadn't actually damaged anything of his. "Meanwhile, you can let her go." Quinton didn't really want her in jail. He just needed Jennifer to leave him and Callum alone.

"Then I suggest you go home and stay there. We will need to report this incident to Child Services, and the courts will ultimately decide the custody of your child." Man, Wyatt's eyes were like steel. "If it were up to me, I'd take you in and book you again, but it seems that Mr. Jackson is nicer than I would be." He stepped back, and Jennifer sent him an icy glare before taking a few steps.

"No matter what you think, you aren't going to take my baby. I'll see to that." She then stalked away.

"Thank you all. Would any of you like some coffee or water?" Quinton asked.

"No, thank you," Kip answered. "If she gives you any more trouble, just call us. She definitely isn't doing herself any good. We will be filing a report on the incident. Just call in tomorrow to get the number. That way you'll have it for court."

Quinton thanked him, and the two officers got in their car and drove off in the same direction Jennifer had gone.

"Are you still on duty?" Quinton asked Wyatt. "I can put on some coffee or something." He didn't want to be alone right now. Part of him was concerned that Jennifer might come back. Jennifer was a strong person, and she had a way of getting what she wanted.

"I can stay for a little while," Wyatt agreed, and Quinton opened the door. "I guess she was pretty angry." The plexiglass in the lower part of the door was spidered and cracked with a few pieces missing.

"Jennifer seems to think that she can get whatever she wants by bullying." Quinton was glad it was quiet. "Give me a minute. I need to make up a bottle for Callum." He hoped that would calm him. He went into the refrigerator to get a bottle and warmed it, then checked it was the right temperature before giving it to Callum, who ate, his eyelids drooping in seconds. "I had just gotten home from picking him up when she started banging on the door, and it scared him." He didn't go into how her blow to the door sounded like a gunshot.

"I'm glad you called," Wyatt said. He followed Quinton back into the living room, where they sat down.

Quinton loved feeding Callum. He had his son's undivided attention, and most of the time he watched him with those intense blue eyes before closing them as the bottle soothed him. This time he was ready to relax, and slowly Callum's sucking slowed. He wasn't all that hungry but had mostly needed comfort.

"Hopefully it isn't going to take too long before the initial hearing. Cases that involve children are usually prioritized."

Quinton nodded. "But I bet there are going to be multiple hearings and plenty of questions and home visits, stuff like that."

Wyatt nodded. "I also need to tell you that the court is most likely going to do its best to reunite Callum with his mother. It's the way these things work, especially with a small child like Callum. The law presumes that the mother is best to care for children." He smiled at the baby and leaned closer to look at Callum.

"I figured. I'm glad that the police have records of her behavior. It will make things much easier to show the kind of person she is and what she's capable of. It's bad enough that she left Callum in an unattended car and that he was taken, but now we have her violent behavior and witnesses. People who are reliable." God, at least he hoped so. The thought of giving up Callum made his heart sink. He knew it was a possibility, but….

"All you can do is be the best parent you can and be able to demonstrate that to the court." Callum opened his eyes, and Wyatt smiled and offered his finger. "He's going to be a really strong boy, I know it."

"Thanks for coming. I wasn't sure what to do, and I had your card, and...." He slowly got up. "Would you hold him?"

Wyatt easily took Callum in his arms, and Quinton got a couple mugs of coffee and brought them in. Callum looked good in Wyatt's arms, and since Wyatt was watching the baby, Quinton took a few seconds to watch Wyatt. He was strong and had great eyes and a high, chiseled jawline that gave him an almost model quality. But it was his smile and the gentleness that seemed to radiate from within that most captured Quinton's interest. Well, that and the fact that Wyatt was just hot. No two ways about it, Trooper Wyatt was smoking. As he looked his fill, Quinton remembered that he was just standing there, and he sat down, which gave him a chance to cover his rising excitement. Not that Wyatt had shown any interest in him in that way. Hell, Quinton didn't even know if Wyatt swung his direction— like it was going to matter anyway.

"You did the right thing. She was determined, and you needed reliable witnesses to her behavior." Wyatt spoke softly. "This little guy is pretty amazing. I love how trusting he is."

Quinton grinned. "He isn't like that for Jennifer. With her, he's fussy, cries, and refuses to sleep. She complains about him all the time. But for me he's as good a baby as I could hope for." Callum chose that moment to spit up all over Wyatt's uniform shirt. Quinton jumped up and got a cloth for Wyatt, then took Callum to wipe him up as well. Then he settled Callum on his shoulder with a burp rag while Wyatt unbuttoned his shirt.

"Let me rinse that out or else you'll end up smelling like baby spit-up and formula." His mind slipped a track as Wyatt handed him the shirt, now wearing only a skintight T-shirt. Man, he was fit and muscled. "I'll be right back."

"Give him to me," Wyatt said, and Quinton handed over Callum, who settled right against Wyatt's chest. Quinton wished he could nuzzle up against him like that. Dang, that would be amazing.

Pushing the idea from his mind, he took the shirt, rinsed it out in the sink, and then put it in the small dryer off the kitchen. The appliances were one of the few areas the landlord had spent some money, so the washer and dryer were relatively new and worked well.

When he returned to the living room, Callum was asleep in Wyatt's arms, and a stab of jealously went through him. Quinton knew he was being stupid—jealous of his baby. "Can I ask you something?"

Quinton nodded, stiffening a little from Wyatt's tone.

"What happened when you were a kid? The person I know now doesn't seem like the kind of guy who stole from stores and did things like that."

Quinton shrugged and thought about his answer. "It would be a cop-out to say that I was a loser magnet and that the people I hung around with pulled me down the wrong path, because that isn't exactly true. I fell in with them because we thought the same. We all had nothing and didn't see why we shouldn't have what everyone else had. I really thought that way and took what I wanted." He paused. "But basically I didn't care because I didn't fit in anyway… being gay and all." There, he'd put it out there, and he watched Wyatt closely for a reaction. What he got was a slightly wicked smile that had Quinton's heart beating a little faster and his belly fluttering in that possibly knowing way. "It was Nancy who took me aside and told me she was disappointed in me. That she knew I could do better. If she hadn't, I don't know where I'd be today. But it would probably be behind bars or something. I was always good with my hands, and she helped me get the job at Dickinson in their maintenance department."

Wyatt nodded. "You decided to pull yourself up."

"Nancy read me the riot act, and she can be scarier than Jennifer, let me tell you." He smiled as he thought of his sister. "She was always there for me, and I see now that she did her best even when she was away. I didn't know Nancy was lesbian until a few years ago. They kept it quiet, I guess, because they live and work in North Carolina, home to stupid bathroom laws. Not that it matters, of course. She and her wife are happy, and they come back to visit about once a year."

"What did she think about the whole Jennifer thing?" Wyatt asked, and Quinton rolled his eyes.

"She thought I was being stupid. But Mom was pressuring me to be 'normal.' Apparently Mom thought that having a lesbian daughter was enough, and me being gay was just too much for her. Jennifer was nice, and we'd met a couple of times when I'd gone out and stuff." Quinton felt the heat in his cheeks growing. He used to drink a lot more, and there were times when he didn't really remember shit. Not his finest hours, that was for sure. "She seemed interested, and I had already had a few beers, so I took her home and we spent a couple hours together. It wasn't special, and drink was most definitely involved. I guess I was able to do my duty, because Callum was the result. But it did bring into focus that my interests lay in another direction."

He watched as that knowing expression made an appearance. "All I remember from when she told me was thinking how an idiot screwup like me was ever going to raise a kid. At first I figured Jennifer would put it up for adoption or something. But she wanted to keep the baby, and I was in no position to argue with her. I pay child support because Callum deserves a chance. But…." Now he wondered what the money was being used for. "Like I said, I compounded dumb on top of stupid. I should have just stood up and been who I am in the first place." Quinton lifted his gaze from the floor. "So that's me in a nutshell."

Quinton expected to see pity or even disgust in Wyatt's eyes. Not that he'd blame him for either one. Instead, he rocked Callum slowly as Quinton tried to decipher his expression. "You know, it takes a pretty strong person to make a change in their life. I see it all the time. People make the same mistake over and over again. They do the same thing and expect something different to happen. You saw what you were doing, admitted it, and have tried to put your life on a different path. That's hard."

"Callum deserves that," Quinton said. "I knew while Jennifer was pregnant that I was going to have to get my act together. Nancy helped me as best she could. I had my job, and I made sure I put my energy into it and did the very best I could. The college is training me so I can become a registered plumber. I'm good at it, and I work with some pretty awesome guys."

"Did you ever have trouble at work because you're gay?" Wyatt smiled at Callum, who was now asleep in his arms.

Quinton reached for his phone and snapped a picture. "One of the guys gave me some shit. The supervisor and the guy who's training me, Jeff, gave him hell, and he almost lost his job. The college takes stuff like that really seriously." He took a deep breath and tried to figure out how to say what he wanted, but the words sounded wrong in his head. Finally he just pressed ahead. "What about you?" If he was wrong, he could plead stupidity.

"The department has had nondiscrimination policies in place for years, and I've never had any trouble. I think there are some troopers who have a problem with gay people—there always are in any group—but mostly it has been a nonissue for me. I guess I'm lucky. This part of the state can be a little problematic."

Quinton leaned forward. "Do you worry that one of those guys won't have your back or something?"

"I guess… maybe." Wyatt swallowed and tensed. "There are plenty of things I worry about. But I'm the same as the other troopers, and I treat everyone with the same respect that I feel we all deserve. I've had a few weird comments made from time to time, but mostly it isn't a big deal for anyone." He shrugged. "I guess that concludes the coming-out portion of the evening." He grinned, and Quinton sighed.

"There's nothing wrong with being up-front about things, I guess. Jennifer hates that I'm gay, in case you hadn't guessed. I'm the father of her baby, and I think she thought she had gotten her hold on me good, so when she learned I was gay, she got really angry."

"Do you think she was trying to trap you?" Wyatt asked.

It was funny, but the thought had never occurred to him before. Maybe it should have. Quinton shrugged. "I don't know. She always lived beyond her means. Look at the Lexus she was driving. But if that's what she was trying, it didn't work out for her. She talked about getting married, but that would have been a recipe for disaster for both of us… and for Callum. I knew that." He sighed. "So now the mother of my son hates me."

"So what?" Wyatt said. "Maybe being with Jennifer was a mistake, but you didn't compound it."

Why was Wyatt being so nice? Quinton couldn't quite figure out why an upstanding guy like Wyatt, a cop no less, would want to have anything to do with a loser like him. Bad decisions followed him like ducklings after their mother. Wyatt didn't deserve that. Heck, Callum didn't either, but he was his son, poor thing, and there was nothing anyone could do to change that. "You don't understand. If there's a mistake to be made, then I'm sure I'm going to take that path."

The last thing that Quinton expected was for Wyatt to laugh. "Does this little guy look like a mistake?" He stood up and gently passed Callum back into his arms as the dryer buzzed. "I'm not particularly religious, but my adoptive parents are, and Mom always says that some things are just meant to be. Our path may not make sense to us, but it's leading us all somewhere. And maybe your path led you to him." Wyatt gently stroked Callum's head and then rested his hand on Quinton's shoulder.

Quinton turned, and his gaze caught Wyatt's. For a split second, everything else slipped away and he lost himself in his deep eyes. There was something enticing about him, and Quinton licked his lips, wondering what Wyatt's full mouth would taste like. He leaned nearer, stretching to cross the distance between them. Wyatt drew closer, and Quinton's eyes closed a little, and he held his breath in anticipation of a kiss that didn't come.

"I'll see you tomorrow in class." Wyatt smiled and then straightened up and left the room. He returned with his shirt on, doing up the buttons.

"We'll see you."

Wyatt said goodbye and left the house.

"That was interesting," Quinton said softly to Callum, who stretched without opening his eyes. Quinton wasn't sure what to make of all that. He certainly wasn't going to get his hopes up, but he liked Wyatt. The guy was decent, strong, and honest. Part of Quinton felt like he didn't deserve someone like that. Lord knows he hadn't been any of those things in the past.

His phone chimed, and Quinton checked the message. *I'm out front. Let's do something.* It was from David. Quinton hadn't had time for friends in a while. He carefully put Callum in his crib and went to answer the door.

"Hey," he said quietly.

"Dude, where have you been? The guys are going to Alibis tonight. They have a drink special and live music. We all wanted to see you, so I thought I should drop by and get you to come have a drink… or five." He grinned. David was always up for a party.

"I can't," he said softly. "I have Callum, and he's asleep."

"Why not call Jennifer and have her come pick him up? Or just take him back to her and we can all have a good time." It smelled like David had already started the party. His breath reeked of cheap whiskey.

Quinton wrinkled his nose. "Because I have Callum for now. She…." He hesitated to tell David what was going on. He had opened up to Wyatt after knowing him just a few days, but he still wasn't totally comfortable telling David about himself… and he had known him for four years. "Jennifer wasn't taking care of Callum properly, so I have him now, and the courts will need to decide what happens going forward."

David shook his head. "Why fight it? Just let her raise the kid. You pay your money and then you can go on with your life. Johnny has some really good shit. After we eat and have a few drinks, we're going over to his place. Remember that party last summer? It's going to be like that." He was all excited, but Quinton didn't feel the same way. Last summer he had been all about the party. Heck, that was how he and Jennifer met and why things got carried away.

"Because I'm his father," Quinton answered.

David shrugged. "I got myself a kid or two out there somewhere. Maybe. I don't know. It doesn't matter to me. The mother takes care of the kid, and I get to go on with my life." He smiled as though things were that simple, and damn, it was like a mirror being flashed up in front of Quinton's face. He couldn't imagine acting that way, especially now that he had a three-month-old baby who depended on him.

"I can't. Maybe another time. You and the guys have fun, but you'll have to count me out. I need to stay here with Callum." He was already moving David toward the door.

"I know—I'll call the guys and we'll move the party here. That's a great idea." He already had his phone to his ear.

"No, David."

"Hey, Johnny, I'm at Quinton's, and I got a great idea since he has his kid." David ignored Quinton. Quinton's first instinct was to just go along. That was what he'd always done. "That's what I was thinking. We—"

"No," Quinton told him firmly and pulled the phone away. "Ignore David. No party here," he told Johnny. "I have Callum, and I can't have a house full of people. You all have a good time." He handed the phone back to David, who seemed stunned. "I'm serious."

As if to punctuate the point, Callum began to fuss in the other room and then cry full out. Quinton went in and got Callum out of the crib, changed him, and carried him back out. "I'll see you guys later. I need to feed him and get him bathed and ready for bed."

David made a fish mouth at him. "You'd rather stay here and take care of a baby than come out with us and have a blast? Is there something wrong with you? What kind of man are you? Let Jennifer or your mother take care of the baby. Jesus." He threw his hands in the air and rolled his eyes. "We're your friends— "

"Yeah. Obviously, you're my friends…." He shook his head and opened the door. "I'll see you next time." Callum fussed more loudly. Quinton did his best to soothe him, but he was hungry, and only a bottle was going to quiet him for very long. "I'll see you later."

He ushered David out, closed the door, and threw the lock. "Come on, sweet boy. We're going to go get you something to eat, and then you get to have a bath. You love baths." He bounced him and got a prepped bottle from the refrigerator, warmed it, and gave it to Callum, who sucked on it like he was starving.

Quinton didn't want Callum to go to sleep right away, so he kept him awake, and as soon as he was done with the bottle, he took him into the bathroom and filled the special bathing tub Nancy had sent with warm water. Once again he sent a thank-you out into the universe for his sister as he placed Callum in the tub. He grinned and splashed a little while Quinton got him washed. The heat in the water didn't last long, so as soon as he was done, Quinton wrapped Callum in a blanket and got him nice and toasty. Then he diapered him and put on his pajamas.

Of course Callum was wide awake now, so Quinton let him play with his favorite toy for a little while, made up another bottle, and then settled him in his arms. Quinton had never been particularly musical, but he sang softly as Callum had his before-bed snack, and once he was out, Quinton put him in his sleep sack and into the crib for the first part of the night.

Quinton stood in the doorway, watching his child sleep. Those rosy cheeks, the little mouth that sucked even now…. Callum was probably dreaming of huge, magical, never-ending bottles. All Quinton could think about was how much this little guy had changed his life. He closed the door partway, went into the next room, and turned on the television at low volume. It wasn't even nine o'clock and he was already in for the night, had put Callum to bed, and was doing nothing more exciting than watching television.

Quinton wondered what his friends were doing. Probably already on their way to either getting drunk or flying high. Maybe both. That had been his life a year ago—actually less than that. He wasn't going to reminisce about the good old days or some such rot because he had something better. As soon as that thought flashed through his mind, so did an image of Wyatt on the sofa in his muscley T-shirt, holding Callum in his arms. Quinton wanted to be held and cared for too. But it was the way Wyatt looked at Callum and, a few times, him. Even the memory sent a warmth running through him that he couldn't explain, but he wanted more of.

Well, Quinton had learned some time ago that what he wanted and what he got were two very different things. He settled in to watch television to maybe rest a little, because Callum was going to be up and would want another bottle in a few hours.

# CHAPTER 5

WYATT FELT like crap. No, that was wrong. Saying he felt like crap would be insulting to those who actually felt like crap.

His day started out with him oversleeping and having to race to get ready for work, and had ended in a fiery crash on the freeway that he'd arrived at just in time to hear the screams of the people inside the car before it became a fireball. Those panicked screams, abruptly cut off, had been playing in his ears for the past two hours.

A hot shower and a snack revived his body, but the sounds kept replaying in his mind and wouldn't stop. He came to class hoping for something to take his mind off it.

Wyatt took the same seat he had the last time and kept looking for Quinton at the next one, which was empty. He checked the clock and then the seat again, hoping somehow that Quinton had made a miraculous appearance. Next, he checked the door as it opened. The instructor came in and the door closed, cutting off an unhappy cry from outside.

Wyatt got up and went to the door. When he opened it slightly to peer out, he saw Quinton with Callum in his arms, trying to soothe his unhappy baby. "He's not hungry or wet. I just changed him, but he doesn't want to be comforted." Quinton looked about at the end of his rope.

"Hey, little guy," Wyatt said and took him from Quinton. Callum blinked at him and stopped crying. "Did you just want someone else? Is that what this was all about?" He smiled at Quinton. "How are you doing otherwise?"

"He was up most of the night and just got to sleep about two, then a few hours later I had to wake him to take him to day care, and that started the whole fussy baby routine." He lifted the carrier and diaper bag, and they went inside as Wendy started class.

Callum stayed quiet and dozed in Wyatt's arms. However, if he moved to put him into the carrier, Callum fussed, so he held him and finally managed to get the little guy asleep enough that he could settle him in the carrier without waking him.

"Now that's an example of teaming up," Wendy said. "Sometimes young children just want a change of scenery, like the rest of us." She grinned. "And after all, who wouldn't want to be held by Trooper Wyatt back there." The class tittered. "There are times when children and babies just want something we can't seem to give them, and since they can't talk, we have to learn to figure things out." She continued, and Wyatt sat back, a little worried about Quinton, who seemed about ready to fall asleep in his chair.

Still, he managed to stay awake through the entire class and took some notes. Once Wendy dismissed them for the night, Wyatt gently lifted Callum's carrier, and they walked out into the warm night. "Have you eaten?" Wyatt asked.

Quinton shook his head. "I managed to change clothes after work, and that was about it."

"Then follow me to my house. I have some things there I can make." He handed Callum to Quinton and went to his car in the lot. He drove slowly until Quinton pulled up behind him. Then he led the way home and parked on the side of his tree-lined street.

"THIS IS really nice," Quinton said once Wyatt had welcomed them inside.

"Make yourself comfortable," Wyatt said.

Quinton sat on the sofa, lifting a wakening Callum out of his carrier. He fussed a little and settled on Quinton's shoulder.

"I have bottles and things with me," Quinton said.

"Does he need one?" Wyatt asked.

"He took one just before I left the house, and I was hoping that would settle him. He quieted while he had the bottle, then refused to sleep and just fussed until someone with the magic touch got him to sleep." Quinton settled on the sofa as Wyatt went to the kitchen. He had some pasta sauce that he'd made and put in the freezer, so he got it out and put water on the stove. He also got out some bread and spread it with garlic butter, getting it ready to go in the oven.

The quiet gave him a few seconds to himself, and Wyatt realized he hadn't thought about the accident— but of course as soon as it returned to his mind, it came back full force.

"Callum seems to want to look around," Quinton said, pulling Wyatt out of his thoughts. "Is something wrong?"

"Just a difficult day," Wyatt answered. "I responded to an accident on the highway, and it was pretty bad." To say the least. He swallowed hard. "I know there was nothing more that I could have done, but it's still hard. I got to the scene just a moment before the car burst into flames." Wyatt figured there was little more he could say. He didn't want to tell Quinton too much about the accident itself. There was no need for him to have those thoughts in his head too.

Wyatt turned back to the stove, and Quinton gently rubbed his shoulder with one hand. "I wish there was something I could do to help."

Quinton was already doing it. Wyatt stilled, soaking in the comfort of the gentle touch. It had been a while, and he closed his eyes, trying not to pull away. Quinton wasn't going to hurt him. Wyatt told himself that again and again in his mind. Being touched didn't mean pain and hurt. Or at least it didn't have to. He released a deep breath and forced the initial tension out of his muscles.

"You are so very tight, Wyatt. It's like you carry all your tension in your shoulders."

"I'm okay."

Quinton stopped the movement of his fingers but left his hand on Wyatt's shoulder. "Your muscles are firing like nobody's business." He tugged gently, and Wyatt turned around. "You know it's me, right?" He pulled away. "If you don't want me to touch you, I won't. I was only trying to help. It sounded like a bad day."

"It was really nice of you." He smiled, telling his overreacting mind that everything was okay. Thankfully, the initial reaction wore off and he was able to get control of his feelings and body once again. "I'll be okay. Unfortunately, shit happens in my line of work, and I have to deal with it."

Quinton snorted, and Callum squeaked a little before settling. "You've helped me with my huge pile of crap, but you won't accept help in return?"

Wyatt knew how it seemed, but he had never been one to share his troubles. They were his to deal with. Maybe that came from the years in foster care. If you were a troublesome or fussy kid, you got shuffled from place to place. But if you were good, quiet, and no problem, then you got to stay, and maybe the family you were with would want to keep you. At least that was how it had seemed to Wyatt. Not that the family that had adopted him didn't love him, or that he didn't love them and owe them the world, but that was how it felt. It was hard to let things like that go.

"You don't need to deal with my stuff," Wyatt said as he turned back to the stove. The water had started to boil. He gave it a few moments before adding the pasta.

"I see. I would have thought we were friends of some sort, and that's what friends do." Quinton sounded disappointed and maybe a little hurt.

Wyatt didn't like that. "I suppose it's like being a doctor. You hate to lose people, and I keep thinking that if I'd been faster and had gotten there a little quicker, I might have been able to help them."

"Or you could have gotten caught in the fire yourself," Quinton told him. "Sometimes stuff happens for a reason. At least that's what my mother would say. I don't know if she's right, but maybe it's true. I personally think that things happen because they do, and getting wound up over what we can't control is kind of futile."

"Well, thank you for listening. There isn't anything anyone can do. I just need to process this, but it's good of you to listen." He stirred the pasta and put the garlic bread in the oven, then checked the heat under the sauce.

"You really are strong, aren't you?" Quinton sat down. "I've known a bunch of guys in my life, and it's the ones who think they're strong who won't let anyone help them."

"It's not like I need help." He set the spoon in the holder. "Sometimes I just wonder why stuff happens. I got to the scene and could see they were in trouble, but there was gasoline spilling out of the car. I called for fire equipment, but it only got there in time to put the fire out." *Not in time to save the two people inside.* "It's the stuff where you can't help that hurts the most."

Quinton scratched his head. "I can understand that." He paid special attention to Callum.

"It seems like he's settled down."

"That's because you're his new favorite person. When we go home, he'll fuss and fight me all night again. It happens sometimes. Then something will change again, and he'll only want me and no one else will do." He sighed. "Maybe he wants Jennifer, and she isn't here to comfort him. I really don't know." He met Wyatt's gaze. "Does it make me a bad person that I'm happy she's a bad mother and that it gives me an opening to raise my son?"

Wyatt didn't know how to answer. "I don't think it makes you bad, but it does present problems. Let's say you go to court and you win custody of Callum. She can keep petitioning for some sort of visitation or even shared custody if she gets her act together. I've seen it multiple times."

"Yeah, I know. The courts keep wanting to re-unite the child with the mother." He sounded defeated. "What chance do I really have?"

"That's up to the court. You might want to contact Donald to find out what's happening. I can give you the names of some of the child advocacy groups. They might be able to help you with legal assistance." He knew there was nothing he could do in that area and suspected that Quinton had very little money.

Wyatt checked the food and drained the pasta, sending up a cloud of steam. He added the farfalle to the sauce and gently stirred it together before filling a couple of plates and placing one in front of Quinton.

"This smells amazing. Did you make the sauce?"

"Yeah. Go ahead and start while it's hot. I'll get the garlic bread." He set his plate at his place and got glasses of ice water before getting the garlic bread on the table.

Wyatt's phone rang, and he picked it up as he sat down.

"Hey, Donald, what's going on?" He took a bite of pasta. It really did have a great depth of flavor.

Quinton was eating with Callum in his carrier, awake and looking around.

"A call from Jennifer Winters came into the hotline about fifteen minutes ago. The call log details her information. She said she was invited to a party by some of Quinton Jackson's friends yesterday, and it's apparently spilled into today. He hasn't been home all day, and she thinks that he's there with the baby. Before I contact her…."

Wyatt snickered. "It seems her imagination is getting the best of her. Quinton and Callum are sitting right across from me. Callum is having a bottle of what I can only guess is nummy formula, and Quinton is eating pasta with some of my homemade sauce. And he wasn't home because he was at the parenting class you signed him up for. This is the second time she's tried to cause trouble. The local police have a report of the other night when she tried to come to the house. I was there as well. Please get a copy and add it to your case." He could almost see Donald smiling through the phone.

"I will, definitely."

"Maybe a psychiatric exam should be recommended before she has contact with Callum. Though that needs to be your call. The other night she was wild and kicked in Quinton's storm door." He asked Donald to hold on for a second. Wyatt smiled as he leaned across the table. "What did your landlord say about the door?"

"That he was turning it in to his insurance company, and they could go after her for damages. I made sure my landlord had her name and address. He's a really nice guy. Before I had Callum, I did a lot of work on the place myself, and he took it off the rent." Quinton bit his lower lip, and Wyatt nodded, holding up a finger to let him know that he'd tell him everything as soon as he got off the phone.

"The information about the broken door should be in the report. Her behavior is really starting to make me wonder." Donald asked Wyatt to put the call on speaker, so he set his phone on the table and enabled that option.

"Quinton, I wanted you to know what's happening. We're going to document everything. Our case has been filed, and I suspect that we'll have an initial hearing as soon as possible, probably in the next week or so, to determine placement."

"What does that mean?" Quinton asked. "That I'll know then if I get Callum?"

"No. This is a drawn-out process. No quick and lasting decisions will be made early. This initial decision is for Callum's placement while the hearings move forward. You have classes next week, and I'm going to schedule a visit by one of my social workers. Her report will be used by the judge as well. If you need anything, don't hesitate to call."

"Are you doing things to help Jennifer too?" Quinton asked.

"I'm here for Callum. That's my primary purpose, and that means making sure you have what you need to properly take care of him. The courts will decide who takes care of Callum going forward. My department will make a recommendation based on our visits and what we know about both of you. So, Quinton, you want to make a good impression."

"Okay. So you aren't on my side," Quinton said.

Wyatt patted his hand, enjoying the touch. "Donald and his people are on Callum's side. That's how they work. They want and will argue and fight for what's best for Callum."

"I want what's best for Callum too," Quinton said. "And if that's Jennifer, so be it. But I don't think so."

"Then we are on the same side," Donald said rather flatly. Wyatt figured it was his professional demeanor coming forward. Donald was an amazing person, but professionally, he could be cold. Wyatt was privileged to know that was only a defense mechanism. "But I will tell you that you're doing the right things, and I'm glad you've held up your end of the deal so far."

Quinton shook his head. "Callum is my son, and he's the only one I'm ever going to have. Of course I'm going to do the best I can for him. And as far as any deal is concerned, you all make sure you hold up your end, because I'll fight Jennifer and you if I have to in order to keep my son and make sure he's safe and grows up with a chance at a better life than I had." Determination rang like a bell in Quinton's voice. Wyatt knew Donald had heard it too, and that was probably part of what Donald was hoping for.

"I'm sure Quinton will be notified of the hearing date and that he'll be ready for the social worker." Wyatt figured he should bring this to a close before these two got into a dick-measuring contest or something. The fire inside Quinton was good to see, and he had made his point, but Wyatt figured that was enough. "I'm sure he appreciates everything you've done to help."

"I do," Quinton agreed.

Wyatt ended the call and took a bite of his dinner.

"Really, like I'd take a baby to a party where people are drinking and getting high." Quinton rolled his eyes.

Wyatt held his gaze. "You need to understand that Donald sees some of the worst things where children are concerned. He and his husband have a son they adopted. Basically, his husband and his partner on the force found him locked in an attic. The boy had been mistreated in ways that would make you sick. He's a sweet boy, and because of Donald and Carter, he has a good life." Quinton's complexion turned a faint shade of green. "I'm only telling you this so you know where he's coming from."

Quinton reached for his water. "Okay. I guess I can understand that. But I'm not going to let anything happen to Callum."

"I know that," Wyatt said gently. "And you're on the road to convincing Donald, I'm sure of it." Quinton's hand shook, and Wyatt squeezed it.

"I thought you didn't like being touched," Quinton said as he looked down at their hands.

Wyatt wondered at how quickly they had returned to that. "You startled me before. I wasn't expecting it, and…." He closed his eyes, groaning. He hadn't meant to give away that much information, and yet Quinton had pulled it out of him with ease.

"Something happened to you," Quinton stated. "You don't have to tell me about it. Everyone has a right to their privacy." He turned his hand over and threaded their fingers together. "But it's no sin to ask for help either. You're willing to give it at a moment's notice. So take it when others offer."

Callum seemed to be drifting off, so Quinton released Wyatt's hand and gave Callum a bottle. He drank for a few minutes and then closed his eyes and was out.

"You don't understand. Any sort of weakness can be used against a foster kid. You have to be strong and take what comes silently, and…." His throat ached.

Quinton's eyes widened. "You think I don't know about being strong? My mother brought home men all the damned time. Some were decent, but most were losers. I had to deal with them, the kids at school, and the stronger kids who wanted what little I had. I know what it means to need to be strong. But I also had friends to back me up. They weren't the smartest of friends, and yeah, I got into trouble, but without their backup, things could have been a hell of a lot worse. I needed them to survive, and that's what I did for a long time. It's what you did when you were a kid too. You just got lucky and ended up with people who loved you. I had to grow up pretty much on my own."

"You had Nancy," Wyatt said, and Quinton nodded.

"She's probably why I'm not in prison right now like Anthony. He stole a car and then held up a convenience store. He and I were supposed to go out that night, but I was sick with the flu or something. I stayed home, and he got sent up. I suppose I was lucky that night. I dodged a bullet, and it sort of woke me up a little. That's when I asked Nancy for help... and she was there." His eyes seemed watery, and for the first time, Wyatt felt like he truly might have found someone who understood what he was carrying around. That didn't mean he was ready to talk about it yet, but maybe he was a step or two closer to being able to open that closed and locked portion of his mind.

"Let's finish eating before the little stinker wakes up."

IT SURPRISED Wyatt how easily his life and activities with Quinton seemed to meld around Callum and his schedule. They managed to finish eating, and Wyatt was taking care of the dishes when Callum gave a loud cry that had Quinton snapping to attention. He went to change him, and Wyatt put the dishes away and sat on the sofa. When Quinton returned, he sat next to him, holding Callum. Without thinking about it, Wyatt leaned close just to watch him.

"I sometimes can't believe how much babies sleep," Wyatt whispered.

Quinton snickered at him. "I've thought that too, but what else are they going to do? Run a marathon?" He grinned as he shook his head. "I guess babies have one job: to eat, sleep, and poop so they can grow. I mean, he's already so much bigger than he was when he was born."

"Were you there?" Wyatt asked, and Quinton shook his head. "I see."

"Jennifer wanted her mother there, and I can't blame her for that. I had already realized that she and I weren't going to be anything other than friends. She was still pressuring me for more, but it wasn't going to happen. So her mother with her for the birth seemed like the right thing to do. I wish I could have been there, but then I might have had to spend time at the business end, and...."

Wyatt laughed and had to try to control himself. "You already did. How do you think you got Callum in the first place?" He had to quiet himself as Callum fussed and waved his hands. Wyatt moved his hand closer, and Callum grabbed his finger and held it. He began to doze, so Quinton settled him in his carrier.

"Yeah, okay. I did once. But that doesn't mean I wanted to again." He bumped Wyatt's shoulder and then seemed worried. "Touching you doesn't bother you, does it?"

Wyatt stifled a groan. He should have done a better job of covering his discomfort. "No, Quinton. It was just that I didn't see it coming. That's all. And you don't need to worry or feel sorry for me."

Quinton shrugged. "I don't. We all have stuff to deal with, and why should you be any different than anyone else? Pity sucks, if you know what I mean. But I want you to feel comfortable."

"I do," he whispered, and Quinton looked toward him. Wyatt found himself drawn nearer, and Quinton licked his lips, the tip of his tongue just making an appearance. Wyatt hesitated for a second, holding Quinton's gaze. He could look into those deep eyes forever, and every time he inhaled, Quinton's manly scent with a hint of spice made his head feel lighter and sent little zings up his back. "I feel comfortable with you."

"Me too," Quinton whispered, his full red lips moving slightly. Wyatt licked his own lips and drew even closer. He half expected Quinton to look away or for Callum to decide at that moment that he was unhappy, but none of that happened. On the wall in the dining area, his grandmother's clock ticked its unchanging rhythm, but even that seemed to slow down. Wyatt took a chance and raised his hand, placing it on Quinton's slightly stubbly cheek. Wyatt thought about asking if that was okay, but Quinton didn't pull back, and he didn't want to break the moment. "Wyatt...."

He tensed. "Is something wrong?"

"Definitely not," Quinton whispered, and Wyatt closed the distance between them. His lips were firm and perfect. Quinton added his own pressure, responding to Wyatt and then pressing even harder. Wyatt closed his eyes as he and Quinton went on a gentle journey together.

Quinton pulled away, and Wyatt slid his eyes open, his mind still reeling from the kiss. "Everything okay?"

"More than." Damn, he could feel his cheeks heating like he was in school again. Wyatt kissed Quinton again, this time more gently, but with the same urgency. He needed to do this, and God, Quinton tasted good. He had this deep, rich flavor that drew Wyatt in and made him want more. When they pulled back, he was breathing hard.

Quinton's eyes shone and sparkled. When Callum fussed, they both looked down. Quinton adjusted the bottle, and Callum instantly settled and went back to feeding.

"Wow," Wyatt breathed. "That was...."

"Yeah," Quinton breathed. "Look, I need to get Callum home so I can put him to bed. Otherwise his schedule will be completely off and the poor day care people will have to deal with another grumpy-baby day." No one wanted that.

"Okay," Wyatt agreed, and they got up off the sofa. "I'm off on Sunday. It's supposed to be a nice day. Maybe we can take Callum out for a walk in the stroller."

"That would be nice," Quinton said before transferring Callum to the carrier and getting their things together. They shared another kiss at the door, and then Quinton went out to his car. Wyatt waited until they were gone before shutting the door. Being with Quinton seemed to make the ghosts of his past run for the darkness, and that was good, though he wondered how long he could keep them there.

# CHAPTER 6

"Is THERE anything else you need from me?" Quinton asked as he sat in one of his old living room chairs, holding a sleeping Callum and trying not to look too nervous, even though his dinner kept threatening to make a reappearance.

"No, Mr. Jackson," the social worker, Rhonda, answered.

"Please, call me Quinton," he corrected. "I feel like I've been saying this a lot, but I want what's best for Callum." That was enough to keep his attention where he needed it. Well, that and the knowledge that on Sunday, he'd be seeing Wyatt again.

Rhonda cleared her throat. "Well, if all my home inspections were like this, my job would be easy. The house is clean, and you have enough supplies for Callum. While he doesn't have a room of his own, he does have a proper crib, and he's close to you. As he gets older, that will need to change, but for now, keeping him close to you is for the best. I see that you have day care."

"Donald helped arrange it for me," Quinton said. "He's also helped me with diapers and those kinds of supplies. Though I have adjusted my budget for those things in the future since I won't be paying child support. The hardest thing for me is day care. I can't afford a thousand dollars a month for that on top of everything else. I just don't make enough money." He bit his lower lip.

"That's okay. We see that a lot and have a program to help you. Donald has already entered you in that program, and you qualify based on your income. However, you're currently listed as provisional because of the upcoming hearings."

"Is there anything else I need to do?" Quinton asked.

"Not that I can think of. Like I said, if all my home visits went this well, my life would be so easy."

"Wyatt—Trooper Nelson—said it should be good." He flashed his best smile.

"My only area of concern is the stairway to the basement. Before Callum becomes mobile, there's going to need to be a way to block that doorway. People sometimes put up baby gates, but those are only so successful. Maybe you can talk to your landlord. Also, I noticed the front door…."

"Jennifer, Callum's mother, kicked it in when she couldn't see Callum. The landlord is taking care of it." He wished all her questions could be that easy.

"What about other child care besides the day care?" Rhonda asked. "Not that it's part of my report, but I thought I'd ask. Everyone needs the occasional evening out. It's part of keeping your sanity. What about your family?" She seemed so genuine.

"My sister doesn't live in town, and I don't really spend time with my mother." That was the safe answer. "I've been spending time with Trooper Nelson—Wyatt—and we're seeing each other tomorrow. Callum thinks he's the best thing since bottles." He smiled, and Rhonda nodded. "Jennifer was always complaining that Callum was fussy and cried a lot. But I find him pretty happy."

Of course Callum chose that moment to start fussing. Quinton excused himself, got him changed, and made up a bottle, with Rhonda watching from the background. Then he sat down to feed him. "Would you like to hold him?" he asked at the longing look in Rhonda's eyes. "Sometimes he just wants a change of scenery." He put him in her arms, and Rhonda fed him with a smile. Quinton didn't say anything, but the pain in Rhonda's eyes had him wondering what might have put it there. Not that it was any of his business. "He'll take about half the bottle and need to be burped." Quinton got a cloth, and when it was time, he took him and lightly rubbed Callum's back until he did his impression of a sailor.

"I need to be going." She left a card on the coffee table. "Let me know if you have any questions, and I'll file my report in the next few days. You can get a copy by contacting the department." She headed for the door. "I can let myself out."

Quinton breathed a sigh of relief once she was gone, the tension draining away.

His time feeding Callum was quiet time. He didn't watch television or anything. Callum had his attention. Quinton knew that regardless of what happened in court, Callum was going to grow up fast and these hours were going to come to an end. Someday Callum wasn't going to need his father to feed him anymore. Eventually everything else would slowly slip from his control to Callum's and their time like this, just the two of them, would become more and more rare. Quinton tried not to think too much about it.

Quinton kept Callum awake for a while after his bottle, letting him play with his toys. He liked it when Callum was active and alert. It didn't last all that long, so he made the most of it. Quinton was learning that baby laughs were the best sound ever.

A pounding on the door startled Callum, and he fussed immediately. "I'm sorry, buddy," Quinton said as he picked him up and went to the door. "David."

"It's another Saturday, and all you do is spend time here at home. I brought over a pizza and thought we could hang out for a while." He breezed inside and set the box from a local place on the coffee table. Quinton checked the sidewalk before closing and locking the door. David rarely showed up anywhere alone. Usually he was part of a group.

"I'm going to need to give Callum his bath and then put him to bed in a few hours." He wondered just what David had in mind. He put Callum back down to play. "I have some things to drink in the refrigerator."

David went to the kitchen and returned with a couple of Cokes. "No beer?"

Quinton shrugged. "Can't afford it anymore. That money needs to go to diapers and formula." Not that he needed to be drinking. That was a common factor in his stupid decisions.

"You're turning into an old man," David cracked as he flipped open the lid on the pizza box. Dang, the scent wafted over and his stomach rumbled. Quinton grabbed a piece and took a bite while he watched Callum.

"I'm a father," he told David. "I know it seems strange, but I have to do what I can for him." He settled back on the sofa. "You remember how it was when we were growing up. Our parents had their own stuff to do, and we all ran wild. I don't want that for him. He deserves better—hell, *we* deserved better." He hoped he was making his point.

"Man, you really have changed." Quinton wasn't sure if David was sneering at him or not. "We're your friends and we can't even see you. On top of that, you're spending all your time hanging out with cops." He made a yuck face. "You know how those guys are."

"Yeah, I do. They helped me when Callum was in the back seat of Jennifer's car when it was nabbed."

David snorted. "That was a joke. Didn't you hear? Caleb took the car to scare the crap out of her for leaving it running with no one in it." He took a bite of pizza. "Then this guy chased him all over town and out onto the freeway. Caleb thought they were after him because he isn't the smartest bulb on the string. You know if you chase him, he will run. Then he was nabbed by the cops."

"And Callum was in the back seat. Was he so stupid not to realize that it was my car chasing him?" Quinton tossed down his pizza. "He could have killed Callum, the way he was driving."

David leaned forward. "You gotta help him."

Quinton shook his head. "I can't have anything to do with him. No way."

"What kind of friend are you?" David demanded. He was really pissed off.

"You need to keep your voice down." Quinton glared at his friend. "Is that why you stopped by? Did you finally get the story and put all this shit together? And you figured that if you talked to me, I could get Caleb off the hook? Well, I can't. If Jennifer doesn't want to press charges for taking her car, that's her business. But Child Services is involved for him being taken, and the whole incident only highlights that she's a bad parent for leaving him alone in the car in the first place. He's going to have to fight his own battles. I have enough of my own right now." Shit, this was getting really complicated. He needed some advice—*legal* advice—and he needed to call the numbers he'd been given for help.

"That's just it. Caleb didn't know Callum was in the car," David whined. "And now he's in jail, and you could help him."

Quinton leaned forward. "But I can't. The law is involved, and *they* brought the charges against him. *I didn't*. Meanwhile, I need to take care of my son. He was the one who was put in danger because Caleb and Jennifer managed to compound dumb on top of stupid." He stood. "If this is all you came for, then take the pizza and just go. I have to think of Callum. That's all that matters, and whether Caleb meant to or not, he kidnapped my son and endangered his life. Period. He needs to think about the shit he's doing. We all do." It really was time to fucking grow up, and if his friends couldn't do that, then so be it.

"Hey, hey, cool your jets." David put his hands up in surrender. "Damn, don't get all aggravated and shit. I've never seen you this way. You always just went along with what everybody did and had a good time." He picked up his pizza and ate once again. "You know, a backbone looks good on you."

"It would look good on you too, ya know. Spending our lives in the slow lane isn't going to get us anywhere. I have a good job now, a kid to take care of, a place of my own." David was still living in his mother's basement with her taking care of him, for God's sake. She still cooked his meals and did his laundry. "We aren't kids anymore, and the mistakes we make will stay with us for a long time." He sighed. "You have a good job working for the county. But you still live at home and spend all your cash either at the bar or with the pot dealer. How long are you going to do that before you realize you've pissed away thousands of dollars that you could have used to buy a house and have a better life? Think about it. We didn't have much growing up, but that was then. We get to decide what we want now." Quinton picked up his piece of pizza again and stepped down off his soapbox. "Thanks for the pizza, by the way. It's good. It's been a long time since I had something like this."

David nodded. "Can I ask, what's with you and the cops? Steven and Caleb think you're selling everyone out on everything they ever done."

Quinton rolled his eyes. "See, dumb. Wyatt saved Callum and has helped with him. He's nice, and I like him." He wasn't sure how that was going to go over. "Wyatt's good, and he's stable, and he really seems to like me. I like him too. He even knows about the stupid things I've done. The guy saw my record when he pulled me over, and he's still coming to see me. Callum really likes him too." He glared at David. "So what's the big deal? Am I supposed to run the people in my life through the moron council of Steven and Caleb? If that's the case, then fuck them." Man, he was getting angrier by the second.

"Hey, Jesus. I was just asking." He really didn't seem to get it. "I guess things have changed."

Quinton paused to think. "Yeah, I guess they have. The decisions I make aren't just for me anymore." He went to check on Callum and turned to find David right behind him.

"The little guy is cute, isn't he?"

Callum had his face turned their way, lips sucking, hands squeezing and relaxing.

Quinton backed away from the door frame. "David, he's everything. I know that's hard for you and the guys to understand, but it's true. Callum is more important to me than partying, than anything else." He partially closed the bedroom door so the light didn't shine on Callum.

"The little stinker is really cute and all. But are you really prepared to be his parent and take care of him for the next eighteen years? You know he's not going to remain that cute or that quiet. Soon he'll walk and then talk, and after that, there's no stopping him." David chomped on his pizza, and Quinton wondered what was coming next. "Aren't babies better off with their mothers?"

"Were we?" he countered. "My mother went about her business and left me to raise myself. Yeah, she had some basic rules, but after that she was off drinking most every night down at Alibis, and I was supposed to be a good little boy and stay at home. We all know how well that turned out." He finished his slice of pizza and picked up another one. "When it came to parents, we got the booby prize. That isn't going to happen with Callum." He swallowed and drank some soda. "Why do you care so much?"

That question seemed to come out of the blue, and David didn't have an immediate answer. "Because I'm your friend, and…."

"Friends respect their friends' decisions," Quinton reminded him.

"But things will never be the same." David seemed to deflate like a popped beach ball. "They can't be, can they?"

"Now I think you're starting to get it. We aren't kids anymore, and acting like it is only going to make us those pathetic middle-aged people who dress like teenagers and look something like Krusty the Clown." He knew he was exaggerating, but what the heck.

"When did you get so smart?" David challenged.

"When I became a father," he fired back. "When I found someone more important than I am." He finished the second slice of pizza and his soda before sitting back on the sofa to relax. "You have no idea how good this feels. I haven't had anyone over other than Wyatt since I got Callum, and it isn't that often that he's quiet like this." He stopped himself. "That's enough about me. What's been going on with the rest of the guys? Other than Caleb. There really is nothing I can do for him."

"Well, I've been listening to Jennifer bitch about you for days. I swear, dude, she wants to rip your balls off." He grinned. "But there's nothing you can do about that either."

"Nope." He leaned forward. "Let me ask you this. Would you want her as your mother?"

It took about two seconds for David to shake his head. "Okay, okay, I get your point. But I'm just saying."

"I already know, and so does the front door," Quinton added. "It doesn't matter what she thinks. It's going to be up to the court, though I know I don't have a huge chance there. They always want to return the child to the mother. Especially a baby. But I want to give him the best chance I can."

"You may not get that chance. Jennifer was saying just yesterday that if she gets the baby back, she's going to move away from here. Her family is outside Philadelphia, and she wants to move there to be close to them again and to get away from you. I don't know how serious she is, but that's what she said."

Quinton had known that was a possibility, but still it chilled him to the bone to hear it. Just another reminder that he really needed to contact the legal people and get some help.

"Thanks," he said just as David's phone went off. He could just imagine that it was one of the other guys trying to find out if David had been successful. But it didn't seem to be, and David jumped to his feet. Quinton showed him to the door while he continued talking a mile a minute about some sort of delivery. He didn't want to think about what David was up to now. It was none of his business, and Quinton had plenty to worry about on his own.

THANK GOODNESS it was Sunday. Callum sat happily in his little bouncy chair, grinning like crazy. The chair was the most recent present from his sister, and Quinton had called to thank her. "He loves it," Quinton told her.

"I knew he would," Nancy said, "and we have some news. I'm pregnant."

"Oh my God!" Quinton said gleefully. "That's amazing." Then he started to laugh. "You do realize the last time I heard those words...."

Nancy snickered. "Yes, but we have been trying for a baby. And you got one by accident. So how is Callum otherwise?"

"Growing like a weed and eating me out of house and home." He carried the phone through the house and let Wyatt inside.

"Was that him? The hunky trooper?" Nancy said loudly enough that Wyatt heard.

"Yes. Trooper Hunky, at your service," Wyatt retorted, and Quinton fake groaned.

"You better get in here before your head won't fit through the door, and Nancy, be good," Quinton scolded lightly. "Or have your pregnancy hormones already gotten the better of you?" He laughed as she sputtered. He knew if he'd said that face-to-face, he probably would have gotten smacked.

"Hey, you were the one who said he was hunky."

"And he is, but he doesn't need to hear that," Quinton told her.

"Yes, I do, and as often as possible," Wyatt said.

Quinton shook his head. This was like playing telephone tennis, and the game was over as far as he was concerned. "I'm hanging up now. Wyatt and I are taking Callum out for the afternoon. I'll talk to you soon, and thanks for everything. Also, I'm thrilled about being an uncle." He disconnected, still smiling. "Nancy's pregnant, and they're thrilled. I guess it just took a little perseverance."

"That's awesome," Wyatt said, tugging him into a hug and kissing him hard... literally.

Quinton wondered what it would take for them to have a quiet day in. Maybe they could spend some time while Callum was napping....

"Are you two ready to go?" Wyatt asked.

Quinton motioned toward the kitchen, where Wyatt made a big deal over Callum before lifting him out of the chair, to more happy coos. "He's in a good mood today. I have the diaper bag all ready, and the stroller base is by the front door. I just need to get him in his baby carrier and we're all set." He let Wyatt put Callum in the seat, and once he'd gotten him strapped in, he lifted him, and they headed for the door.

The two of them took Quinton's old car because the car seat was in place and moving the thing was a real pain. "Where are we going?" Quinton asked.

"Well, there are lots of places to go hiking and things, but that isn't going to work with Callum, so I thought we could head over to Letort Park. I got a table already set in the shade."

Quinton handed Wyatt the keys and let him drive to the park.

Wyatt pulled into the lot and parked just as his phone rang. He answered it and immediately stiffened. "Yeah… okay…." He swallowed. "Okay, I'm on my way now." He hurried out and grabbed what he had been using to hold the table. Then he pulled out of the park. "I have to go to work. There's a situation outside of town, and it's bad." He continued driving until he pulled up in front of Quinton's house. "I'm really sorry. I'll be back as soon as I can. I promise." He got out of the car, hurried over to his, and took off.

Quinton sighed and pushed his disappointment aside. He'd really been looking forward to some time with Wyatt, but there was nothing he could do. He got Callum and carried him inside.

# CHAPTER 7

IT WAS as bad as Wyatt had feared. "Do you have any ideas about this?" Captain Harker asked.

Wyatt stood just outside the end of a buried semi-trailer that had been acting as a secret drug distribution center. Evidence was being gathered inside, and it swarmed with half a dozen troopers and crime scene specialists going over the container with a fine-toothed comb. When they'd stormed it, two officers had been shot, along with one suspect. Unfortunately, the leaders had gotten away, and the suspects they had in custody weren't talking. "No. That's the crappy thing. I didn't have an inkling that this kind of thing was here."

"And we wouldn't if some kind of fight hadn't broken out. They hid what they were doing really well." Captain Harker scratched his head. "It took some resources to put this together. Tomorrow I'm assigning you to run this down and see who might have arranged for this." Wyatt nodded as he took notes. "I'm making you the point person for this. You've wanted a chance at an investigation—well, here it is."

Wyatt grew excited. "What else do you need me to do?"

"Nothing at the moment," Captain Harker told him. "I know today was supposed to be your day off. Go on home and enjoy what's left of the day. Tomorrow you can go over everything they find and get started."

"Thanks," Wyatt said and hurried away before someone changed their mind. It was late in the afternoon, but maybe he and Quinton could salvage some of what he had planned.


WYATT DIDN'T want to knock too loudly in case Callum was asleep. Instead, he texted Quinton that he was out front and waited. Quinton's old car was still in the same spot he had parked in before leaving, so he hoped Quinton was at home. He checked his phone, but there was no reply.

Wyatt knocked softly on the door. He heard footsteps from inside, but no one came to the door. Maybe Callum had just gotten up and Quinton needed to take care of him. He messaged again and knocked but didn't receive an answer. There was nothing he could do, so he turned to leave and just head home when Quinton turned the corner, pushing the stroller.

Quinton strode toward him. "Are you done?"

"Yeah. I sent you a message," Wyatt said.

Quinton dug through the stuff in the pocket of the stroller. "Sorry. I shoved everything in there. Callum was getting fussy, and I hoped a walk would get him to sleep." He slowly rocked the stroller back and forth.

"Is there supposed to be someone in your house?" Wyatt asked.

Quinton shook his head. "Of course not." He started forward.

"Okay. When I knocked, I thought I heard footsteps from inside. Give me your keys and please stay here. I want to check just to be sure." It was possible he was wrong, but his instincts had kicked in.

Wyatt stopped at his car and got his gun from the lock box in the trunk. Then he returned to Quinton's house, unlocked the door, and slowly pushed it open.

He listened for movement and checked each room of the house. It seemed quiet, and he didn't discover anyone inside. Still, something niggled at him. He had heard someone inside; he was sure of it.

Wyatt checked the back door. He pulled it open and checked the area around the lock. There were scratches that seemed fresh, like someone had tried jimmying the lock. Since he had a key, he went out and tried to do the same. With enough pressure on the lock, it released and the door opened for him. That wasn't confirmation that someone had been inside, but it bothered him.

Wyatt went inside and closed the door before returning to the front and getting Quinton.

"Is it safe?" he asked.

"Yes. But I need you to look around and see if anything has been moved, and check the back door. Someone might have come and gone that way." He helped bring in the stroller and lifted Callum out. Callum snuggled right up against him, and Wyatt loved that closeness.

Quinton went through the house, checking each room before moving on. When he got to the back door, he checked it over and then closed it again. "I don't know. The back door looks the same, but I never paid that much attention to it. I don't see where anything has been moved." He continued looking over each room and rubbed the back of his head. "I just don't know. Why would someone break in and not take anything? Not that I have all that much, but the TV and other things are still here."

Wyatt shrugged and then wandered into Quinton and Callum's bedroom. He made a circle of the space. The bed had been made, and the crib was ready for Callum to use. He lifted the sleep sack and paused as a small plastic bag with koalas printed on it fell out of it. "Quinton," he called softly, not touching it.

"Yeah." He came into the room and must have followed Wyatt's gaze. "Shit," he breathed. "That isn't mine." Quinton paled, and his hands shook.

"I know." Wyatt thought back to when he'd been here before he'd been called into work. "Remember, you got the diaper bag and I followed you into the room. Callum's crib looked just the same as it did just now. Other than that." He pointed. "I think someone was in the house, and they planted that in the crib." It didn't take him long to figure out what was going to happen next. He pulled out his phone and made a call.

"Kip, I need a favor," he said once the call was answered.

"What's up?" Kip asked.

Wyatt explained everything. "Okay, I find this, and it's too easy a setup. I expect an anonymous tip will be called in very soon. Is it possible to have someone come over here and have this bag printed?" He knew in his heart that Quinton would never hide pot in Callum's crib. Whoever had planted it there had done a really stupid job of it. He had a pretty good idea who might be behind it.

"Sure. I'm in the area and will stop by in a few minutes."

Wyatt ended the call and carefully handed Callum to Quinton. Then he met Kip out front and led him to the bedroom.

"You called that one right. A call came in just a few minutes ago, and they were a little too specific about what we might find and where." Kip took possession of the bag and looked over the baby bedding, even smelling it.

"This hasn't been there very long. Otherwise the bedding would pick up the smell." He set down the bedding and turned to Quinton. "I have to ask if you have any idea how this got in your baby's bedding."

Quinton shrugged. "Of course not. Wyatt said he thought he heard someone moving in the house when he knocked on the door. I've been out of the house for the past hour taking Callum for a walk. He was fussy, and I needed to try to get him to rest." He sat in the living room, soothing Callum, who did not appreciate having his nap interrupted.

"Okay, I get that." Kip pulled out his notebook. "Who might want to do something like this?"

"Jennifer is the main one. She's Callum's mother, and she probably thinks discrediting me will help her get Callum back. After that I have no idea. Unless it's some friend of hers out of some misguided loyalty. I really don't know. It doesn't seem like anything was taken, so I guess someone broke in here to leave me a little unwanted present."

Kip nodded. "Can I ask what you would have done if you had found the pot and Wyatt hadn't been here?"

Quinton swallowed. "I would have called him, and if I couldn't get hold of him, I'd have flushed the entire mess." He looked downtrodden. "I used to smoke the stuff with my friends. But that was before I got Callum. Heck, my friends have invited me to parties and I haven't gone. I'm not going to take a baby to something like that."

"Okay, Kip. I think we need to figure out who did this. Let's run it for prints and see if we get anything. And we need to run an analysis on the pot itself. Maybe it can tell us something." Wyatt was interested to see where it came from and if it matched anything else known to be circulating in town. The baggie itself was nondescript and completely ordinary except for the koalas.

"Okay. I'll get on it. Carter is back in the station tomorrow, and this sort of thing is right up his alley. But I'm going to need to put together a timeline of the afternoon."

Quinton snickered. "That's pretty easy. Wyatt and I were going to go on a picnic to the park, but he got called, so he brought me back here. After that, I made lunch and played with Callum for a while. He was fussy, so I put him in the stroller and walked him around for about the past hour. I came back, saw Wyatt in the area, and…." He drifted off, and Wyatt took over, confirming what he could.

"Did you see anyone you knew on the walk?" Kip asked Quinton, who shrugged.

"Not really. A few people stopped to look in and coo at Callum, but other than that, it was just a baby walk. He fell asleep, and I wanted him to rest, so I kept walking, even after my feet began to hurt a little. Then I turned the corner and saw Wyatt." He actually smiled as he said the words, like now that he was here, everything was going to be okay.

"Kip, do you really think that Quinton put pot in his baby's crib and then invited a cop into his house to look around?" Wyatt cocked his eyebrows.

"As I said before, no." Kip closed his notebook.

Wyatt took Kip out to show him the back door, and they looked through the small yard. There was no indication that anyone had been back there. No telltale footprints in the mud or anything. Not that Wyatt expected any. "It would be pretty easy for someone to come and go without being seen through the backyard and then the alley."

"I thought so too." Wyatt paused at the edge of the blacktop. "Quinton is going to try to fight for custody of his son, and Callum's mother is in hot water. I suspect that this is an attempt to plant something bad on him to try to even the playing field."

"Yes. It looks like something like that. But you have to admit that Quinton doesn't have a spotless record. And unless we can figure some way to prove that this stuff was planted, it's going to raise some sort of doubt. I'm glad you called, because you aren't impartial in this. I'll do my best to try to find out who might have done this, but you have to know it's going to be difficult to come up with a definitive answer unless we get really lucky." Kip didn't seem too hopeful, and Wyatt knew he was right. Still, they had to try.

"I know. And thank you for all your help." He was going to need to figure out this puzzle, because the alternative was that Quinton would lose Callum—and that was something Wyatt wasn't going to allow to happen.

Wyatt began walking back toward the house.

"I've got to ask," Kip began. "Do you really believe what Quinton said in there? That he's turned down the chance to go to parties and that he's changing his life because of the baby? It seems like a lot to believe." He didn't seem snarky, but even so, Wyatt felt defensive.

"Why not? He had a crappy childhood, and he wants something better for his kid. Quinton's holding down a job and has for a while. He wants his kid to have a chance. That's a good thing as far as we're concerned." Wyatt also explained about the tip to Child Services to bring the point home. Still, he understood why Kip was skeptical. They heard things like that all the time, and it usually turned out to be untrue. "Give him a chance."

Kip nodded. "I guess. I mean, that stuff was so obviously planted, it's ridiculous. And the call that came in that said that he was hiding his drugs in his baby's things. Whoever tried this sure as hell did a terrible job." He chuckled. "We'll find something, if for no other reason than the fact that they're so inept." He put his notebook away. "I'll see you later, and I'll let you know when we have anything." Kip went through the house, and Wyatt followed, finding Quinton on the sofa, holding Callum.

"They're going to take him away, aren't they?" He lifted his gaze, eyes filled with misery. "The report will get back to Child Services, and they aren't going to care if someone put that stuff there. They'll have to take him just because it was there and they don't know why." He lightly patted Callum's diapered butt. "I'm trying to be a good father and do the stuff I wished my mother had done."

"They aren't going to take Callum," Wyatt said and yanked his phone out of his pocket. He scrolled through his contacts and called Donald.

"What's going on?" Donald answered. There was laughter in the background. It sounded like they were having a kids' party.

Wyatt kept the story as brief as possible. "I called the local police, and they agree this looks like a setup, especially with the fishy phone call, which was recorded." Maybe they could identify the voice—Quinton might recognize it. "Anyway, I wanted to let you know rather than through some other way."

Donald chuckled. "You really like this guy, don't you?"

"Is that so bad?" he asked.

"God, no. It's a really good thing. Brings out your protective instincts." Sometimes Donald saw way more than anyone had a right to.

"What's that supposed to mean?" Wyatt demanded.

"It means that you're on the phone to me to make sure we know what happened because you care for the guy and want him to be happy and are worried about him." Wyatt glanced over to where Quinton sat with Callum. "It's a cop thing. You're all the same."

"Excuse me," Wyatt said, to Donald's laughter.

"Don't get all pissy. It's good. Why do you think I married Carter? He's the exact same way. The guy can be as nice as anything, but if someone just looks at me or Alex, he'll get protective as hell." He continued chuckling. "Tell Quinton not to worry. I'll look over the report when it comes in and make sure that all the facts are included. Though I do have to tell you that this is going to be problematic. Regardless of what you find out, this will come up in the hearing because it has to."

Wyatt nodded. He knew that was true. "Then we're going to have to have clear and provable answers."

"Yes, exactly." Donald returned to his party, and Wyatt put his phone in his pocket. Now he had to figure out how he was going to make sure that this little family stayed the way it was. Callum was happy, and in his heart Wyatt knew that Quinton would never do anything to harm him or put him in danger. Someone had it in for Quinton, and Wyatt was going to prove who it was… period. But he had to do it before the hearing, or Quinton was going to be in trouble.

"ARE THEY going to take Callum?" Quinton asked after sitting on the sofa for a good half hour, just holding his son. Wyatt could feel the pain radiating off him as though it were waves of air over a field of ice. He held his son close, as though he expected Donald and an army of social workers to descend on the house at any moment.

"No. Donald knows what happened, and I'm going to work with Kip to prove it. I'm going to get a copy of the call that came in. The tip may be anonymous, but maybe the voice isn't. Then we're going to check for fingerprints and see if the drugs themselves can tell us anything. It was obviously a setup. Donald knows it."

Quinton lifted his gaze, eyes filled with bone-deep fear. "If you weren't here…." The knowledge of what would happen was written all over his face. "You saved me again." He blinked. "Me and Callum."

Wyatt sat next to Quinton, his reservations and worries about the past picking this moment to rush forward. He knew he should reach out to Quinton like he had in the past, but things between them were getting too intense, and that was when things had gone to shit. "I'll always do the best I can for you." He willed his hands to reach out, but it was like they had a mind of their own.

He breathed deeply as his hands and feet tingled. God, he wished he could stop this.

"Wyatt…." Quinton patted his arm, and he closed his eyes. "Is this one of those 'don't touch me' times like before?" Wyatt nodded, and Quinton pulled away. "Do you want to talk about it?" he asked, concern in his voice.

Wyatt shook his head no. "But I know I have to." He took a deep breath and forced the panic away. "I hate that it hits me at the stupidest times." He reminded himself that James wasn't here, and he never would be again. That he was gone and would always be gone. "I was sixteen, and I fell in love with an older man. He was twenty-four, and damn… I fell for him hard. He understood that I was gay, and he was gay too. James said that I was special, and you have to know how that felt." God, he hoped so.

Thankfully Quinton nodded. "I do know. I would have clung to anyone who said they understood me when I was sixteen." He placed his one hand on the sofa, and Wyatt squeezed it, knowing he had to get past this somehow.

"Well, I did, and it turned out that James was into a lot of things. But mostly he got pleasure through hitting. Not being hit, but doing the hitting. It started off as spanking, but I didn't like it. James said that it was because I wasn't used to it." Wyatt's lips trembled. "I loved him and wanted to make him happy. So when he wanted to tie me up, I let him. Then he blindfolded me, and the spankings and hitting went on." He felt his cheeks heat. "I was so stupid because I just let him do what he wanted, and the longer it went on, the farther things went and the less control I had." He paused. "There is nothing wrong with that lifestyle if both people are willing. I know that. But I wasn't, and I'd lost my voice… my way to say no. It was taken from me without me even knowing it." His hands trembled, and he wanted to stand and pace, but it was like his feet had been disconnected. Just talking about it made it feel like he was back there in some dark pit he couldn't crawl out of.

"You were sixteen. What about your foster parents? Didn't they help you?"

Wyatt sniffed. "Remember what I said about being a foster kid? Don't make waves or cause trouble. Do your best to be good at all times or else they'll move you on. They had adopted me, but I was still living my life the way I always had. It was survival. What if they decided they didn't want me?" He managed to pull himself out of the pit. "So I told them nothing about it. He was the son of one of my adoptive father's friends, and…."

"How long did this go on?" Quinton asked as he squeezed his hand.

"For about six months. My adopted father caught us," Wyatt said. "I was tied up and blindfolded when he came in. It seemed he had been wondering what was going on and went to James's house. He was so mad, and I wanted to die of embarrassment. I swear I expected him to hate me, but he flew at James and broke his nose." Wyatt wiped his eyes. "He got me untied and helped me get dressed and then called the police." It became easier at this point. "My dad stood by me. He made sure James was prosecuted to the fullest extent possible. Once I was dressed and okay, he hugged me all the way home. I swear that was the day I knew he loved me."

"Oh my God." Quinton continued holding his hand. "I don't know how to make this better. I mean, my first instinct is to hold you…."

"It's okay. I'm okay now." His hands and feet seemed more normal, and his vision was no longer tunneled. "It just comes back to me sometimes. Especially when I don't see it coming. James used to love to do things when I was blindfolded, and it scared me. I know James didn't love me and that I was just a plaything to him."

"I see. What happened with the police? Were they rough?"

Wyatt shook his head. "They were so good to me and helped me a lot. It's part of why I became one myself. They did their best to help me, and even set my parents up with a counselor to help all of us. I really expected my parents to hate me because I was gay and because I had let James do what he did. But they didn't. They were in my corner the whole way, including through the trial and sentencing. Even when it came out that James had been filming things." He shivered at the thought that the videos were still out on the web somewhere. "As you can imagine, I'm not particularly proud that I ever let him take advantage of me like that."

Quinton gasped and held Callum a little closer. The little one slept on, warm against his shoulder. "I'm sorry, but you were a kid and he was an adult. He knew what he was doing, and you were just following your heart. That he took advantage of you like that is a real crappy thing to do. And it wasn't your fault. James was using you."

"He did. James was able to get whatever he wanted, and I didn't really stand a chance. He used my feelings for him against me." Wyatt hadn't allowed anyone to get close to him in a romantic way since. The fact was, he could feel himself getting closer to Quinton every time he saw him, and it both scared and excited him. If he wanted any sort of future, somehow he was going to have to get over this tension. Only then would he be able to have a normal relationship.

"Did you do the counseling?" Quinton asked.

"Yeah, I did for quite a while, and most of the time I don't think about it much any longer. It's been a long time, but there are some things that trigger the reaction, and you seem to have experienced two of them. Being touched in an intimate way when I don't know it's coming, and threats to people who are close to me. James used to tell me that my family would never love me if they knew who I was. I found out just how wrong he was, but that was part of what he used for control." That was what he hated most—that James was still affecting him all this time, even after he had gotten onto the force. It really made him angry, and it was time that he stopped letting James have control over his life... and who he could care for.

"Do you want me to stop?" Quinton asked, releasing his hand.

"No. What I want is to try to put James's influence behind me. I hate that even now I can react like he's still there." He turned to Quinton. "And I think you and I might have something special." Wyatt wasn't going to go into his fears. He had already talked enough about that stuff. What surprised him was that he didn't see that pitying look he hated so much. Instead, Quinton's eyes burned with anger, his lips set, eyes hard.

"Where is James now?" Quinton asked.

"He was sent to prison, but he got out a few years ago. There's still a restraining order against him. Since his family lives in New Mexico, I was told that he left the state as soon as he was able to. Which is to say, we got rid of him fast. He wanted to go to his family, so they worked out a deal and transferred his parole out there. Good riddance."

Quinton narrowed his gaze. "You looked him up, didn't you?" Wyatt stared at him, and Quinton did the same in return. "If you think you can win a stare-down with me, you're crazy."

"I'm a cop."

"I'm still going to win," Quinton said without blinking, holding his gaze and leaning closer. "You may as well give up, because I know you probably looked him up on Facebook. Let me guess—he posts pictures of what he cooked on the grill and his dogs."

Wyatt broke their gaze as he laughed. "Muscle shots of himself and beer pictures in the backyard."

Quinton grinned. "I knew you'd look."

Wyatt rolled his eyes. "Of course I did. I'm a cop, and I don't intend to let him sneak up on me ever again. He's on the other side of the country, and I'm happy that he is."

Quinton gently lifted Callum off his shoulder and carried him into the bedroom. He returned a few minutes later and sat back down. "Okay, so you know he's thousands of miles away, and you know that I'm not him. I also am not going to hurt you." He sat down. "And you're looking at me, so there isn't going to be any sort of surprise."

"I see. And what exactly did you have in mind?"

He smiled. "I came here after work to see if maybe we could rescue some of our plans for the day. I still have the picnic things, and while it's too late for lunch, we could have dinner."

"I know. But Callum will be asleep for a while," Quinton said. "So, is there anything else you'd like to do?" He cocked his eyebrows delightfully, and Wyatt cupped his cheeks in his hands. "I like the way you think."

"You do, huh?" Wyatt teased as Quinton drew closer to him. Wyatt knew he had been ridiculous to get all panicky with Quinton. He was a gentle man and wouldn't purposely hurt him. Still, he wished he could better control the moments when he got overwhelmed.

"Okay, are you going to kiss me or contemplate my pores? Because if I had known that's what you were

into, I'd have exfoliated this morning to drive you completely crazy."

Wyatt chuckled and then closed the distance between them. Heat blossomed, even though Wyatt was
determined to take things slow. Confession might be
good for the soul, but he wasn't sure what effect it had
on desire.

He needn't have worried. It bloomed like a flow-
er and attracted like a magnet, pulling Wyatt toward
Quinton. He wrapped his arms around the slighter man,
holding him to him, suddenly craving contact. Wyatt
needed it, like he'd been starved for years and now he
could eat his fill, except this was touch. Quinton was
gentle, holding him, returning his kiss, gently caressing
his back. The earlier panic remained at bay and grew
smaller as Quinton's heat extended around him.

"Wyatt, is this okay?" Quinton asked. His lips were
close to Wyatt's, eyes a few inches away, near enough
for Wyatt to see the green flecks among the sea of blue.
"I don't want you to be uncomfortable."

He swallowed hard. "I'm fine." He didn't want
Quinton to treat him like he was broken. But maybe
he was in a way. Normal people didn't panic because
someone touched them unexpectedly. And it occurred
to him that he had never had a problem on the job. It
was only in quiet, more intimate situations. "Really."

"So it's okay if I do this?" Quinton whispered,
closing the distance between them and kissing him
hard, pressing Wyatt back against the sofa cushions.
"Or this…?" He slipped his hand under Wyatt's shirt,
heat radiating from the touch.

"Oh yeah." Wyatt groaned and closed his arms
around Quinton.

"Don't worry. I know we need to take things slowly and you need to come to trust me." Still, that hand did amazing things to his belly and chest, making trails of heat that seemed to go on forever. Wyatt hated that he just couldn't let himself go and not worry about whether his mind was going to take some weird detour into Panicville.

"You know, worrying about something is only going to make it happen." Quinton held still, looking into Wyatt's eyes. "I can tell that you're worried that you're going to panic again, so it's staying right there in your mind." He backed away, taking the heat of his hands with him.

"Where are you going?" Wyatt asked, a little blinky at the quick change.

"I'm making a point. See, you can worry that you'll get panicky and then you get all tense. Then I have to stop. Or you can just relax." He wriggled his fingers. "And I'll let my magic hands do their best. So what do you want, magic hands or no hands?"

Wyatt smiled and took Quinton's hands in his, tugging him closer. "Let's try for the magic." He hugged Quinton and kissed him, letting go of the worry for the time being. It would still be there, but being with Quinton was wonderful, and he didn't want to think about that. All that mattered were Quinton's sweet lips tingling with heat and the way his hands made Wyatt's skin come to life.

Callum's cries drifted into the room, and Quinton groaned and rested against his chest. "He has perfect timing." He sat up and then got to his feet and left the room. Wyatt sat up as well, sighing to himself. The fussing abruptly stopped, and Wyatt listened as Quinton spoke quietly to Callum as he changed his diaper. "You must be hungry."

"I think we both are," Wyatt said, and Callum began fussing once more. When Quinton returned, he handed Wyatt Callum, who quieted right down, blinking up at him with huge eyes.

"You're his favorite person right now."

"I see. Is that okay?" Wyatt asked.

Quinton scoffed on his way to the kitchen. "Sweetheart, there are times when any parent would give their eye teeth for the baby to stop crying. Just know that could mean that you'll get a call at four in the morning because I've been up all night and he refuses to settle. By that time, I'll try anything." He came in with a bottle, and Callum took it instantly. "Just saying… don't be too shocked." His wicked smile was enticing. "You think I'm kidding. After working all day and then being up most of the night because he won't sleep, that can work anyone to their last nerve."

"Okay, then." Wyatt turned to Callum. "Have you been giving Daddy a hard time? You're supposed to sleep at night so Papa can sleep. Okay?" Callum just blinked at him and continued sucking on his bottle. Wyatt wiped his face with the corner of the burp rag. "In the trunk of my car is the cooler that we were going to use for our picnic. We can have one here right on the floor if you like."

Quinton smiled and grabbed his keys, left through the front door, and returned with the cooler.

Quinton got a blanket and spread it on the floor while Wyatt burped Callum and then fed him the last of the bottle. By the time Callum had been burped a second time, he was all smiles and wide awake. Quinton placed him on the floor with some of his toys, and

Callum had a ball batting the hanging bunny and making the carrot spin in circles.

"I keep wondering what's going to happen. Donald said the hearing is going to be soon, and I keep hoping that things work out. I'm worried about what someone planted in my house and that they have access. What if they break in and try to take Callum or hurt me?" He sat down.

Wyatt opened the cooler and set out the containers. They were still cold, which was good. "Before I leave, I'm going to fix the lock on your back door. And I'm going to look into what we have to do to prove that the pot was planted. If we can, then that not only takes that off the table, but it will shift the issue to Jennifer, since she is the one who benefits most." He'd do whatever he needed to do to keep Quinton and the little squirt in his arms as safe from harm as possible.

# CHAPTER 8

SOMETIMES WYATT confused him. The guy was strong, and a cop, and yet he was afraid of intimacy—well, *some* kinds of intimacy. In other words, he was confusing. Not that it changed the way that Quinton was coming to see Wyatt. The guy had come to his rescue yet again. Quinton knew that the latest episode in the ongoing drama that was his life would have resulted in his losing Callum, possibly forever, if it weren't for Wyatt. He understood Wyatt wanting to be protective—it was part of his job and all. And since Wyatt had opened up about what happened to him, Quinton understood about the whole being touched when he didn't expect it thing. What Quinton kept wondering about was what he could do to help him.

No one deserved to go through life afraid of being touched. That really sucked, especially since Wyatt seemed so hungry for Quinton's touch and always leaned into it. And Quinton loved touching him. He was hot, with a fit, hard body and warm, smooth skin that slid under his hand like silk. Not that he'd had the opportunity to know what silk felt like in real life. But still, he imagined it was something like how Wyatt's chest felt under his hands.

"Hey, buddy, you gonna fall asleep?" Wyatt asked Callum, who was barely batting the hanging rabbit, and Callum seemed to spring awake, watching Wyatt. "Is the food still okay?"

Quinton nodded as he took a bite of the macaroni salad. It was cool and tasted good. "It's really nice."

"I'm really sorry about this afternoon," Wyatt told him. "It's part of my job, especially since the crime took place in my area." He bit into his sandwich, and Quinton watched his lips, resisting the urge to lean forward to kiss him, mainly because he had his mouth full and was really hungry. "But did I tell you that they're going to let me take the lead on the case? If I do it right and solve it, this could get me in line for detective." The excitement in Wyatt's voice was almost childlike.

"Is that what you want?" Quinton asked with a grin.

"Yeah. I mean, I like being a trooper, but I don't want to do traffic duty my entire career, and I think I'll be good as a detective. I'm good at following information trails, and I have this sense for knowing what's real and what's a fake trail. At least I like to think so."

Quinton desperately hoped that was true, because him keeping Callum could depend on it. "Then congratulations. That's awesome. What sort of case is it?" Quinton asked, curious.

"We found a hidden drug distribution point out in the country and rounded up some of the low-level people. But they aren't talking, and I suspect they'll have lawyers and aren't going to say a thing. But we got plenty out of the buried container. It should lead us somewhere. All we need to do is follow the trail."

Quinton tilted his head slightly. "But don't the local police have the case?"

"We are the local police. For over half the state, we're the only police force they have. It's mostly rural areas, so there is plenty of ground to cover. We also work with local departments, which is why I know the guys here so well. I work with them all the time. There's often lots of overlap, so coordination and good relationships are key." He gave Callum a tickle and got kicks of his legs and a smile for his efforts. Quinton loved that Callum seemed to like Wyatt too.

Wyatt's phone rang, and Quinton stifled a groan, hoping he didn't have to leave again.

"Don't you guys ever take a day off?" Wyatt said into the phone when he answered. "I see. He's right here. Okay…. I'll tell him. Thanks." Wyatt hung up. "That was Donald. He's been trying to get hold of you and took the chance that I would be in touch with you. He's been trying to call, but you aren't answering."

Quinton hunted for his phone and found it dead. "I need to get a new one, but I can't afford it right now." The danged thing had about an hour of battery before it went dead. Quinton plugged it in, and when the phone turned on after a few minutes, he checked the messages.

"I need to schedule time to bring Callum to the social services center. Jennifer wants to spend some time with him." The idea that she would be anywhere near Callum made him nervous. He knew she was his mother and that she would be supervised, but it still sent the jitters through him.

"You won't even see her. A social worker will take Callum into a visitation room and she'll be with him the entire time. Jennifer will be able to hold and feed him. The social worker will make sure she doesn't try to take him, and she'll observe them together. You'll be in a different waiting room, so bring a book or something to occupy your time for about an hour."

"But… will she give him back?"

"She'll have to."

"But what if the social worker decides that she should keep him?" Quinton's stomach fell through the floor.

Wyatt shook his head. "For now, Callum is placed in your care until the hearing. Jennifer is the one who is going to need to fight to get him back. Her neglect resulted in him being kidnapped." Wyatt hugged him hard. "Just stay calm and be the bigger man. Cooperate and let them know that if there are any issues, you're right there. That's all you can do. Don't try to confront her or even talk to her. The purpose is for her to see Callum, and that's all."

"Are you sure? I mean, Donald put Callum here, but can't another social worker overrule him?" Quinton asked.

"Until there's a hearing, Callum is in your care." Wyatt patted his shoulder. "Just try to relax and not worry about it. So far things are happening the way they should, other than someone breaking into your house and planting drugs in Callum's crib. That's pretty sick, if you ask me."

"Or desperate," Quinton added and took another bite of the salad. It seemed kind of pathetic that he and Wyatt were having a floor picnic and all they seemed to be able to talk about was all the drama in his life. There had to be something else, some conversation that didn't involve the lunacy that his life had become. He lowered his gaze and ate absently, trying not to worry about what was going to happen with Callum. "I'm sorry. This whole thing seems to be the only thing I can think about."

"Of course it is," Wyatt told him, and before Quinton realized it, Wyatt had shifted to sit between him and Callum, his legs brushing his. "He's your son." Wyatt gently touched his cheek. "It's okay. You don't need to feel bad about that."

"And you don't need to worry about having to go in to work." Though he really wished Wyatt had been here. Then maybe someone wouldn't have broken into his house. Though it was likely that they would have whenever they'd gotten the chance. "Do you think someone is watching the house? They had to know when I left so they could get in here. I was gone maybe an hour, and it's not likely that they happened to show up just when I was gone. They must have been watching to know the house was empty." The idea left him chilled to the bone. "What if they're waiting so they can get in and take Callum? If Jennifer is behind all this, then she could take him and leave the state or something. People do it all the time, and then they show up ten years later or something. The kid is grown and doesn't remember the other parent."

"Hey. It's okay. I have a uniform in my car, and I'll stay on the sofa tonight so you and Callum aren't alone." Wyatt hugged him, and Quinton wished to hell that he wasn't so needy and that Wyatt's reassurance didn't feel so good. He could get used to Wyatt being there, and that frightened him. He didn't have the best history when it came to relationships. What if everything just fell apart? Quinton had to rely on himself, and yet Wyatt was right there, supporting him. It felt good to have someone he knew was truly in his corner. Yet he also wondered what was going to happen and how long Wyatt was going to be there. Eventually he'd do something stupid and everything he wanted would be taken away. It had happened before.

"You shouldn't have to do that," Quinton said.

"I don't mind. If something happens, I'll be here."
He finished eating and set the plate aside. "I almost
hope someone tries something. If they do, then I can
get them red-handed and maybe we can put this to bed.
I'd really like some answers about what's going on."

"What do you mean?" Quinton asked.

"I don't know. But Jennifer doing something like
this is too obvious. I'll find out what's going on, but it
just seems like blaming her right off is way too easy
and too pat." He sat back, leaning against the sofa. "Is
there anyone else who might want to get even with you
over something?"

Quinton was a little taken aback. He had thought
that Jennifer was behind this, but now that Wyatt
brought it up, it could be others. The chilling fact was
that he had no idea. He tried to think of someone who
hated him enough to want to have his kid taken away
but couldn't come up with anyone. "I wish I knew. I
mean, Jennifer is all that comes to mind."

"I understand, and I'm not saying it wasn't her."
He picked up Callum and closed his eyes, letting him
rest against his chest. "There's something so calming
about holding him."

"Yeah." Quinton finished his dinner and scooted
slightly to sit next to Wyatt. Their shoulders bumped,
and he tensed before he could stop himself. "Is this
okay?"

Wyatt groaned. "I hate this. You know that?" He
said it without heat. "I know I told you about what happened, and now you wonder if I'm going to go off the
deep end every time you touch me. It isn't like that. I'll
be fine. If something bothers me, I promise I'll tell you
instead of pulling away. Or at least I'll try." He bumped
Quinton's shoulder back.

Quinton turned on the television, keeping the volume low, and changed the channel until he found an episode of *Top Chef*. "I have no idea how to cook like they do, but this show always makes me hungry. I'd love to be one of the judges." He reached for his soda and got comfortable as the contestants set out to cook a main dish with fruit.

"At one point I wanted to be a chef, but I didn't follow it through."

He leaned forward. "Then where did the picnic come from? You didn't buy all this." It was way too good to be store-bought.

"Mom made a lot of it," Wyatt said. "When I told her what I had planned, she said she was cooking and would make some extra for me. She also said that she'd like to have us over for dinner." He seemed really nervous. "I think she wants to grill you to make sure you're up to her standards."

"I see," Quinton said.

"Oh, and of course she wants to spoil the baby." Wyatt grinned. "Mom has been aching for a grandchild for years. Randy is wedded to his career. If he eventually gets married, then she'll immediately begin asking about grandchildren. But right now there are no other prospects."

"You told her about me and Callum?" Quinton asked.

Wyatt nodded. "Of course I did." He paused. "I was a little confused by you. Don't take this the wrong way, but I saw your record, and it scared me. I needed someone to talk with. Mom told me to learn who you were now and to not dwell on the past. She told me it was what she and Pop did when they adopted me. The past was the past, they loved me, and they tried to make the best future for me that they could. She said that people do change, especially when they become parents. So when I called her last, she asked about you and invited you to dinner."

"Well." He didn't quite know what to make of that. His relationship with his mother was strained, and he always wondered what it was that she wanted from him or what her angle was in doing everything she did. "I guess that would be nice." He sniffed a little. "Meeting the parents is a big step." At least he thought it was.

"It's just my mom and pop. Randy is posted at the moment and won't be on leave for a while. He's stationed in Europe right now, so I can't blame him for wanting to travel over there. But Mom and Pop are hopeful that he'll be home pretty soon."

"Have you ever taken anyone to meet them?" Quinton asked. He was trying to gauge how momentous this moment might be.

"No. I never brought home the few guys I dated." Wyatt shifted Callum to his other shoulder, lightly patting his diapered rear end. "My mom will fuss over you like crazy, and I swear you'll probably never get your hands on Callum from the time we arrive until we leave. She has baby fever, and she'll probably spoil him rotten."

"I think he'll survive that. Now I just have to make sure I get to keep him." The thought of Callum going back to Jennifer was more than he could take right now. Yes, she was his mother, but Quinton believed that he was the better parent. "My life is so different, and yet it's the good kind of different. I mean, it seems fuller and better just because I have him. He depends on me, and I never had anyone do that." He smiled. "Before, I think I lived a selfish life, and now, with him, it's better because I live for Callum."

"That isn't entirely good, you know," Wyatt told him. "You need to live for yourself some too."

Quinton shrugged. "I don't have the energy. I work, I pick up Callum at day care, and then my life revolves around him until I get him into bed. And I'm up every two or three hours during the night. That's my life right now." He leaned on Wyatt, who was quickly turning into a kind of rock for him. He really understood why people raised children together. It took two of them just to stay sane.

God, he could get used to this, but Quinton knew he had to resist. Letting himself lean on Wyatt too much would only mean that once he was gone, it would be harder to go back to doing all this on his own. Maybe he was being stupid to hope that Wyatt really liked him. Quinton knew sometimes he was a complete fool—of course Wyatt liked him. Why else would someone like him hang around a screwup like Quinton otherwise? Still, he found it hard to just accept that Wyatt might like him for him.

CALLUM WAS asleep in his crib, and the doors were locked. Wyatt assured Quinton that he had fixed the problem with the back door lock. Quinton got Wyatt some bedding for the sofa, and after cleaning up, he climbed into bed and was asleep in minutes. He used to watch this television show where one of the characters could sleep anywhere in an instant. Quinton now knew that he must have been a father taking care of a baby on his own, because he sure as hell felt like that.

It seemed like seconds, but he woke to movement in the room. He got up to Callum just beginning to fuss. He moved through the house on autopilot, getting the bottle warmed, changing Callum, then settling in the chair in the corner of the bedroom to feed and hopefully rock Callum back to sleep.

"Is he fussy?" a very sleepy, bare-chested Wyatt asked from the doorway, rubbing his eyes.

"No, thank God. He's just hungry. Hopefully he'll eat and go right back to sleep." Sometimes he did, and then sometimes he decided to fuss or that it was play-time. Quinton kept the lights off and was very quiet, creating a soothing atmosphere. "It can be like walking a tightrope. I need him to stay awake long enough to finish the bottle or he'll be up again in an hour, but not too long so he'll just go right back to sleep once he's been fed. I've gotten used to moving through the house mostly in the dark too."

"So everything is okay?" Wyatt asked.

Quinton swallowed hard, because while it was after midnight and all he wanted to do was sleep, one part of him was very much awake. After all, Wyatt was right there with all his sexiness on display, dressed in a low-slung pair of boxer shorts.

"Yes," he whispered, because nothing else would come out. He burped Callum, and then he finished his bottle. After one more sailor burp, he put Callum in his sleep sack and into the crib, where he thankfully settled immediately… which was sort of a miracle. "Go on back to sleep. I'm going to get a drink."

It took all his willpower not to just stand there and ogle Wyatt with all those muscles and that golden skin on display. Even in the low light, there was no hiding the hunkaliciousness.

Quinton got a drink of water and quietly walked back through the house to his bedroom. Wyatt had returned to the sofa, and Quinton told himself he wasn't going to stare, but Wyatt's eyes were closed, and he was only human. He paused and was about to turn to his room when Wyatt held out his hand. Without thinking, Quinton took it, and Wyatt drew him closer and then down.

Wyatt gathered him in, tugging him into a kiss that awakened every cell in him. Before he could pause to think, Wyatt tossed the back pillow-type cushions of the old sofa onto the floor to make a little room, pulling him nearer. Quinton resisted for balance's sake, but gave up the ghost and found himself on top of Wyatt, wrapped in his strong arms. Wyatt slipped his hands under the T-shirt Quinton slept in, kissing as he drew the fabric upward. He paused only long enough to get it over Quinton's head and then drew him back down into the kiss, chest to chest, lips to lips. Quinton groaned softly from deep in his throat. Their legs slid along each other's, sexily rough and tantalizing.

He wanted to ask Wyatt if he was sure about this, but his answer pressed against Quinton's hip, hard, thick, and long, insistent, and damned enticing. Quinton wrapped his arms around Wyatt, holding tight as their kiss grew more intense. The grind was delightful, and he whimpered as Wyatt slid his heated hands down his back and under the band of his briefs, cupping his ass. Fuck, it was amazing to be touched, and Wyatt didn't stop there. The fabric slipped downward, and Quinton lifted his hips so Wyatt could slip his underwear off. With a few kicks, his briefs were gone.

Cool air caressed his skin, contrasting with Wyatt's hot hands, which explored his most private places to incredibly passionate results. Quinton could barely think as instinct took over, and he let it guide him—both of them. Somehow he managed to get Wyatt naked as well, despite the fact that they refused to separate. Heat built and passion grew, driving them forward in a dance in confined quarters that had to be silent, and yet the restrictions only seemed to fuel their need and desire, adding to the intensity, since they both knew things could end with a sound from the bedroom.

"What about…?" Wyatt asked.

Quinton shook his head, then dove down on him for more of Wyatt's luscious lips. The heat built around them, and Quinton held on as Wyatt kissed him harder while their movements intensified. "You know, this sofa is a little small."

"Uh-huh…," Wyatt groaned without letting up for a minute. Short or not, confined or not, none of it seemed to matter, since neither of them could get enough of the other. Hell, Quinton's legs extended over the side, and all he cared about was the way Wyatt touched him, leaving trails of heat that sent goose bumps all up and down him.

"It's also cozy," Quinton whispered, running fingers over Wyatt's strong chest.

"Maybe a little too cozy." Wyatt winked, and Quinton kissed away the rest of his words as energy built between them. It had been a long time since Quinton had been with anyone other than his hand. The last time things had been intimate was with Jennifer, and he didn't want to think about how that had worked out.

"Well, that sort of thing tends to get me in trouble." Quinton trembled as Wyatt rolled over, and within seconds, Wyatt rested on top of him. Quinton parted his legs, and Wyatt settled right between them, his weight firmly delicious and perfect.

"Do you want to stop?" he whispered.

Quinton shook his head. Was Wyatt crazy? Quinton was already half gone, and he held Wyatt's back, sliding his hands downward until he pressed his hands to Wyatt's hard ass. Damn, he must have done squats for days. There was no way Quinton could get enough. Hands, arms, chest—he wanted to touch, taste, and feel Wyatt against him in every way possible. Quinton was almost afraid to close his eyes in case this was a dream and when he opened them again it would be gone. Amazing things like this only happened to him in his dreams, and yet this had to be real. No dream was ever this good or lasted this long.

Wyatt's hands were magic, and Quinton giggled as he tickled his side. He squirmed to get away, but Wyatt leaned forward and licked the spot, sending ripples of rapture racing through him. Wyatt teased and touched until Quinton was barely able to see straight. He gave up controlling the situation and let Wyatt take what he wanted, which was perfect because it seemed that what he wanted was to drive Quinton completely out of his mind… and it was working. He ground his hips upward, needing more friction, and Wyatt obliged, adding his own delicious motion to the mix until Quinton barely managed to control himself. He held on tightly to Wyatt as pressure and desire all mixed together until he could only feel, not think. The pleasure built, tingles raced, and Wyatt kissed him hard, sliding slowly against him, driving Quinton higher and hotter until it became too much. He came between them with a blinding flash, gasping and trying to be silent, with Wyatt following right behind him.

Quinton breathed deeply, not daring to move as he listened for any sound from the bedroom. Callum seemed asleep, thank God. Quinton was still too lethargic to move, and Wyatt didn't show any sign of letting him go. He could stay right here all night if Wyatt let him, but his legs and a gap in the sofa cushion under him had him rethinking that idea. Wyatt gently stroked his cheek and then lifted his weight off him, leaving Quinton slightly chilled after being surrounded by Wyatt's warmth. "Go on back to bed," Wyatt whispered.

"Oh," he said softly, a little confused. Maybe Wyatt had just been horny and let himself go. Quinton got up and went to the bathroom, then closed the door. He grabbed a towel and wiped himself off before getting a drink of water. Then he went to the bedroom and slipped under the covers. Part of him wanted to dissect what had just happened, but the rest of him was simply too tired and worn out. He sank into a heavy but weird, dreamy sleep that featured quicksand or something. Thank goodness he barely remembered it when Callum woke him for his next feeding.

# CHAPTER 9

WYATT WAS exhausted and energized at the same time. Being with Quinton had been amazing, even on that damned sofa of his. There was something to be said for making love in small spaces, but dammit, a king-size bed where he could lay Quinton out and have access to the entire delectable man would be even more enticing. Both Callum and Quinton had been asleep when he left. Wyatt had lightly kissed Quinton, who mumbled his goodbye and then fell right back to sleep. He sent him a text as well in case he didn't remember their parting, and headed in to work.

Today was the first day he was in charge of a case, and he had all the notes to read and wanted to visit the scene again as well.

A great deal of evidence had already been collected and sent off to the crime lab for analysis. It had to be prioritized, and that was one of his first tasks. Crime lab resources were always in demand, and their work was expensive, so he needed the most important items checked first. By the time the initial items had been checked off his list, the troopers who had worked the scene with him began filtering in.

"Congratulations," Mark Whipple said as he sat down at the table in the small conference room. "You're here early."

"Thanks. I need to get up to speed. Did your suspects tell you anything?" he asked, flipping through to the notes.

"Yes and no. Not yet, but I think he will talk. However, I don't think any of the guys working there knew all that damned much. They got their orders through a cell phone. We checked the number, and it's a prepaid phone bought at Walmart. It's been recharged at Walmart using cash. So it's untraceable."

"I already sent the lab the list of evidence to process first, and they said they'd get us what they could as soon as possible." Wyatt looked up as the captain came in.

"I see you're already getting started," he said and sat down. "This is a big deal. The case is already in the news this morning, and we haven't said a thing. News coverage is all over that area, so I sent troopers out to make sure the scene stays secure. You guys need to get out there and see whatever else you need to."

"We're on it," Wyatt told him. "Can we talk to our suspects?"

"I'm working on that. They have attorneys, but I bet they all want to make a deal and cooperate for a lesser charge or leniency in sentencing. That I can handle on my end. You need to find out who is behind this," Captain Harker told him. "We've already made progress shutting down this distribution system, and that's going to help lessen the crap on the streets for a while, but not for long. I'm willing to bet that there are other locations like this all along the I-81 corridor. So with one out of commission, others will take up the slack. Whoever is behind this is probably raking it in, and we need to get to him."

Wyatt nodded his agreement. He had his mission, and he was anxious to get started. "Mark, I'll meet you in the lot in ten." He waited for him to leave. Then he spoke with the captain for a few minutes. Before he left, he sent a message to the lab to bump up the priority on the analysis of the drugs found at Quinton's house. He was stretching to fit it in under his current investigation, but maybe it would help Quinton and Callum. Then he left the station and joined Mark.

"THIS PLACE is a real mess," Wyatt said as he approached the buried container. It looked like someone had used the area as a dump at one point. That would make the container easier to hide.

"It was like that when we found it," Mark told him.

"Then get that out across the agency. These guys tried to hide their work among the debris, so maybe we can use that to find any others." On TV shows, the police always had access to satellite pictures and other imaging. But even if they did in this case, it would be like finding a needle in a haystack. Still, some information was better than nothing at all.

Wyatt walked the perimeter of the container. It had already been photographed and processed. He was hoping for some sort of feeling—something to get his bearings and orient himself so that as the pieces of the puzzle came in, he could put them into place. He made a number of passes, each one farther out than the last. Wyatt came across an especially intense area of trash and cigarette butts, as well as the remnants of product sampling. The smoking station. After pulling on a pair of gloves, he drew a bit of plastic out of the dirt. It was a baggie printed with koalas. "Mark!" he called out. He showed him what he found.

"There were boxes of these inside the container. It could be like the trademark. They probably packed their product in those so their customers would know what they were getting."

"Drug dealers with calling cards." It made a certain amount of sense to him to market a product and build brand loyalty. He supposed if it worked for diapers, why not pot, uppers, barbiturates, or opiates.

"You look like you've seen a ghost," Mark commented.

"I have, in a way." He explained what happened. "I worked with Kip on it, and we're getting the bag fingerprinted. I already authorized it."

"And maybe you got us a real lead at the same time. Whoever placed that with your boyfriend had to have gotten it somewhere, and that could lead us back." Mark seemed excited.

Wyatt's mind was going a mile a minute. "The amount in the bag was at least an ounce, so it was no small outlay. Though the frame job was rudimentary at best. But...." His mind continued spinning. "If you were a regular customer and wanted to harm someone by planting pot on them, would you use an ounce of the stuff? Or would you buy the ounce, take what you wanted to use, and frame someone with a small amount?" He headed back toward the container.

"What are you saying?" Mark asked.

"That whoever got the drugs to try to frame Quinton didn't care about the price or the amount because it wasn't for their use. They broke in and left a full bag."

Mark nodded. "They didn't care what it cost because they didn't pay for it." He grinned again. "So either they were here and had access to this place, or they knew someone who did and they got it from them."

"Exactly. Which could tie what happened yesterday with Quinton to this case." Jesus, he had two ends of the same case from completely different angles. How often did that happen? "Hopefully one end or the other will give us something to go on." He checked around the entrance and then went into the eight-foot-tall container. It was dark as hell. "How did they work in here? There's light from the open door, but not enough to actually work by." He lifted his gaze to the ceiling, where hooks hung down. "Battery lights?"

"Yeah. They stayed off the grid, and I think they did some of their work where you found the bag," Mark explained, and Wyatt nodded. There was very little left inside. Most everything had been hauled in for evidence. He was going to have to look at the photographs if he was to get any sense of the place. "Anything else?"

"No. I was here when they gathered the evidence. I was just hoping that the place could tell me something more when it was quiet. But it doesn't, not really. Though we should keep an eye out in case someone comes looking for something. Normal procedure." He wanted to get at it, so they hurried back to the car. Mark drove while Wyatt checked in and looked through the various photographs.

"I have to ask," Mark said as he drove. "How well do you know this Quinton? Could he be involved in this? I'm not saying he planted the drugs in his own baby's stuff, but obviously he has someone in his life with access. Maybe he's involved or was involved."

Wyatt looked up from the patrol car's computer screen. "If he were involved in shit like this, I doubt that he'd be working in maintenance at Dickinson, trying to scrape by while caring for his son. At the very least he'd have unexplained money, and there's definitely none of that. I know I'm biased, but it doesn't add up. The guy is working as hard as hell to make a life for himself and his kid." Still, as it was, he had difficult questions for Quinton.

"People do a lot to let you see what they want you to see." Mark had a tendency to throw cold water, but Wyatt couldn't argue with him. Still, he didn't think that Quinton had been working to fool him.

"Yeah. But his earnestness about his son...."

"And what would being flush with cash do to change that life?" Mark asked.

Wyatt shrugged. "If he were, his sister wouldn't need to send him diapers, and he wouldn't be eating mac and cheese or clipping coupons for formula. It just doesn't fit at all."

Eventually Mark nodded. "Okay. But when you talk to him, you aren't going to do it alone. I need to be there. If you're involved with him, then it's best if you have a witness to anything he's involved with." Mark was firm, and Wyatt agreed. He needed to protect both himself and Quinton. But Quinton was working, so he and Mark would need to speak with him after he got home.

"I'll agree to that. But you need to keep an open mind."

Mark scoffed as he pulled to a stop at the light at the west end of town. "So do you. This is your first case—your one chance to get noticed and really have a chance to advance. Don't blow it over a boyfriend."

Wyatt didn't agree with that assessment but kept his opinion to himself. As he waited for the light to change, he went back to his computer and checked his email. There was a message from the captain asking to see him, but no updates from the lab. He tried not to be impatient. They handled requests from all over the state, so it was going to take some time before he got anything from them.

His phone vibrated in his pocket as they pulled into the lot. It was his mother asking when he wanted to bring Quinton for dinner. He sent a quick, noncommittal reply, placed his phone back in his pocket, and headed inside.

"I got you some time with our suspects this afternoon," the captain told him as soon as he stepped into his office and closed the door. "The lawyers will be there, and I'll be watching from the other room. You will be the one conducting the interview, but if you get into trouble, I'll have you interrupted with something supposedly urgent to get you out of there. Just relax, and in the meantime, figure out how you want to handle this."

"I think the most important thing is to find out who else in involved. I know we caught these two, but that distribution point was probably manned by more people. They definitely know more than they're telling us."

"Of course they do. But they want to get something for that knowledge. You aren't to promise them anything other than that their cooperation will be noted. We aren't reducing charges, and no one is getting immunity. Everyone thinks this is some kind of bargaining session like on television."

"I know," Wyatt said. "And I was there and saw the areas they were working in. The conditions were pretty bad, so either they were being paid well or they were desperate. If I can find out which, then maybe I can leverage that."

The captain nodded. "I can answer that. These men were rough and looked like they were barely holding it together. My guess is they were working there so they could get whatever it was they needed. So I'd say they fall into the desperate column. Use that."

Wyatt nodded. He intended to use every angle he could get. "Don't worry. I'll be ready to go and on the ball." The captain seemed like he was done, so Wyatt left the office and went back to work.

THE FIRST suspect was in the interview room with his attorney. Wyatt stood outside, took a deep breath, and entered. The suspect turned slightly. His raggedy hair just reached his shoulders. His sunken eyes seemed dull and lifeless.

"Mr. Turner," Wyatt said, and the suspect nodded.

"I'm Regina Beauregard, his attorney," the women sitting next to him said.

Wyatt nodded, sat down, and placed the file in front of him and an open pack of cigarettes in the center of the table. "Do you recognize this place?" He slid over a picture of the inside of the container.

The suspect nodded. "It's where I worked." That was an easy admission. Wyatt also noticed that the suspect paid no attention to the cigarettes.

"And what did you do there?" Wyatt asked. The attorney cautioned her client, but it hardly mattered— Wyatt already had a confession that he worked in the container, and from the looks of the place, he wasn't the janitorial staff.

The suspect shrugged, brushing off the attorney. "I packaged stuff like I was told to." He kept his gaze on the table, hair flopping forward. This was a guy in his late thirties or so who looked like he was in his fifties.

"Why did you work there? What was in it for you?" Wyatt kept his voice level, but with a caring note.

"You don't have to answer," the attorney cautioned again.

Mr. Turner turned to her slightly with another shrug. "I needed to eat, and I needed my stuff." He set his hands on the table. They shook, and he shifted them to his lap once more.

Wyatt wasn't surprised at his shaking. "Do you know this man?" He slid a picture of the other suspect across the table.

The suspect nodded. "He worked there with me some of the time. Lots of times I worked alone."

Wyatt leaned forward slightly. "Was he the only man you worked with?"

Mr. Turner shook his head, straggly hair shifting a little. "There was another man who worked sometimes. When he came, he looked like the rest of us, but he was cocky and seemed to think he owned the place, even though he was a worker just like us. The guy did some of the packaging, but he liked to do it outside for the fresh air." He scowled, and the attorney simply sat there. Obviously Mr. Turner had decided to cooperate.

"But he wasn't working when you were arrested?"

He shook his head. "The guy was never around when the heavy work had to be done. He just showed up when he wanted to." Clearly there was no love lost for this guy.

"Did he have a name?" Wyatt asked.

"Called himself Johnny, but that weren't his real name, because he didn't answer to it until you got his attention. I'm not as dumb as I look, ya know. He was maybe six foot, short black hair, and wore old clothes like us, but he weren't fooling anyone. His shoes were newer, like within a couple months, and comfortable. Not like the rest of us. We sat down a lot because bad shoes hurt. Not this guy. He liked to walk and pace. Jittery, he was." Mr. Turner turned quiet and then lowered his head once again, hair falling forward.

"Was there anyone else?" Wyatt asked, and he shook his head. "How did you get paid?"

"Envelope with our name on it in the trailer every week. Johnny didn't work a lot, but he was there on payday like clockwork. Lazy jackass. Always there first too." He sneered again.

"Did you ever see anyone else?" Wyatt was really curious how the operation could be so hands-off and still function. It wasn't like this was a regular job.

The suspect shook his head.

"How did you get your orders?"

"Through the phone you all took. Texts came through, and we did what he said. If we were on time, we got more money. They kept track of stuff and picked up the orders after we left." Wyatt was beginning to think he wasn't going to get anything more out of the interview when the suspect lifted his gaze, eyes surprisingly clear. "I was working late once to finish up because I wanted the extra money. I was closing up when a car pulled slowly along the road. I thought I had worked too late and didn't know what they would do if they found me, so I hurried out back and hid. Saw them come in and leave with the boxes. Regular-looking guys. On TV the bad guys are always huge, ya know. These were regular guys, and they just walked in and out again. Don't know if it was the bosses or not, but it would be reasonable, ya know."

Wyatt did know and tried to hide his excitement. He asked for any sort of description but didn't get much to go on. He also asked how Mr. Turner got the job, and he said he was approached after he'd asked around because he needed a fix and gave a contact his number. It came via a message on his phone, apparently. Somehow they managed a very hands-off operation, which was impressive.

"They promised me regular pay, and I didn't have any way to eat." Wyatt could have guessed. A desperate man would do just about anything to eat. "Will you tell the court that I was able to help you?"

He met Wyatt's gaze, and Wyatt couldn't help feeling for the guy. "I will make note of your help and make sure it gets to the court." He gathered his files, stood, and made eye contact with the lawyer before leaving the room. He breathed deeply as soon as the door closed. Then he had the other suspect brought in, his mind already leaping to how he could use the information he'd just gotten in the second interview.

"YOU DID good work," Captain Harker told him. "You got confessions out of both of them, and they both described this third man. Unfortunately, it's not much to go on. A vague description and a fake name."

Wyatt nodded. "That's true, but we also have his DNA." He grinned as the captain looked up, expression skeptical.

"That's quite a leap."

"Neither of the suspects we have in custody smokes. I left cigarettes for both of them in easy reach. If they were smokers, they would have sucked one down quickly after a day with none. There were cigarette butts outside under the tree, and this Johnny liked to work outside. Did you also notice the first suspect's description? I'm willing to bet that he was the boss there to see what they were doing. He didn't want them to think too much of him, so he came in disguise. He was also the first one there on payday. I bet he was the one bringing the envelopes. It isn't like they would just leave the money. He would also want to make sure things were working. And he smoked. The second suspect confirmed that."

"I was wondering where you were going. But I see it now." He smiled. "Have some of the cigarettes tested to see if we can get anything."

"They have been prioritized already. But we have to have something to match it to. The problem is that we have little to go on at the moment. Mark and I are going to shake the trees to see if we can get any information out of anyone living in the area. I can't rely on the lab to do all the heavy lifting, so we're going back to basics."

"Let me know what you find," Captain Harker agreed, and Wyatt got back to work.

THE REST of the day was exhausting, with seemingly little progress. But then, a lot of the time, progress came once you'd gathered enough pieces of the puzzle. Wyatt had Mark give him a ride to Quinton's toward the end of the day, and he stood out front for a few seconds before knocking.

"Wyatt!" Quinton said. His expression was happy until he saw Mark. "What's going on?"

"We need to ask you some questions. This is an official visit," he said.

Quinton stood back, and the warm smile slipped away. "I see." He stepped out of the way to let them inside.

"You haven't done anything wrong. But it seems that my case and the pot we found here the other day have intersected."

"The police have it," Quinton said.

"Yes. We know that." Mark took over. "I have some questions that I'd like to ask you. Wyatt agreed I should talk to you because of your relationship. This is for both his and your protection."

Quinton sat down, anxiety rolling off him. "What can I do to help? I don't know where the pot came from, and Wyatt was the one who heard someone in my house. The drugs weren't mine." He bit his lower lip.

"The local police report agrees that the evidence was likely planted. What we need to know is who might have done that." Mark was so professionally cool, and Wyatt could see tension building in Quinton. He wanted to step in front of him to protect Quinton from this entire business, but he couldn't.

"I don't know."

"Is there someone you know who has had a sudden influx of cash?" Mark asked.

Quinton shook his head. "I don't think so." He turned to Wyatt, and then his gaze went back to Mark. "I've had my hands full with Callum for the past week, but before that, I went out with some friends a few times. I didn't notice that anyone was spending money more than normal or throwing cash around, if that's what you mean. Why?"

Wyatt wanted to answer, but he left it to Mark. "The report says there was no small amount of pot found."

Quinton nodded and met Mark's gaze. "I know. It was enough to ensure that I would get into real trouble.

A small amount would probably not be too big a deal. But that bag held quite a bit."

"Yeah. And it cost a lot too. So either you have an enemy who hates you so much that they're willing to drop some cash to hurt you, or…." Mark trailed off.

"Or they have ready access," Quinton finished. "But what does all this have to do with me? That stuff could have come from anywhere."

"It was branded. We know from the bags that it came in," Wyatt explained. "So any help you can give would be appreciated."

Quinton shrugged. "The only one angry enough at me to want to do something like that is Jennifer, and you already know about her." Wyatt could tell that Quinton was thinking, though.

"You need to tell us," Wyatt prompted.

"Well, there was a party the other weekend. You remember, the one Jennifer called Child Services about, claiming that I was there with Callum, which I wasn't. It was apparently a real blowout, from what I heard. Steve tends to have those parties every now and then. He usually gets live music and lots of food, stuff like that. But a party doesn't mean that there's anything wrong going on."

"No, it doesn't," Mark agreed. "Is there anyone else you can think of?"

Quinton shrugged. "If I knew of someone who hated me enough to do what they did, I'd have told Wyatt. I really have no idea who would want to hurt me like this. Jennifer wants to make sure that she gets Callum back, but after her reckless behavior, that's an uphill battle, so making me look bad builds her up."

"Okay," Mark said. "Let's imagine that Jennifer is behind this. Would she have access to what was planted, or would one of her friends? Is she seeing any-one? Maybe she has a boyfriend who got it for her."

Quinton rolled his eyes. "I don't know. It isn't like she comes over and the two of us have hours of girl talk about boys, makeup, and the best diaper cream." He stood and left the room when Callum began to fuss, then returned with him in his arms. "This is frightening to me, okay? Someone broke into my house and plant-ed shit in my son's blankets in order to make me look bad. So now I have to fight harder to make sure that Callum isn't in the care of a woman who allowed him to be kidnapped. He could have been hurt or killed if it weren't for Wyatt and the fact that he took me seriously when he pulled me over." He rocked Callum to soothe him. Wyatt wanted to take the little guy and try to help, but he was on duty and had a job to do. "I go to work and spend the rest of my time caring for him and trying to figure out how I'm going to make ends meet so I can make sure he has a good chance in life. I know you have a case to solve, but I have a son to try to raise, and he's more important than anything." He sighed. "If I knew of anyone who would want to do this other than Jennifer, I would have told Wyatt."

Wyatt met Mark's gaze, trying to get into his head, but he had no idea what he was thinking. "What is your relationship with Wyatt?"

Quinton stopped moving. "Umm, we're friends, and he's been helping me." The imploring expression on his face had Wyatt wanting to jump in, but he had to stay back and let Mark take the lead. If he crossed a line, then he'd step in. "I think he and I are seeing each other."

"You don't know?" Mark asked.

"It's been maybe two weeks. Everything sort of runs together. But he's someone special, and I like him." Quinton's eyes seemed to harden. "Why? Are you the trooper matchmaker or something? Because if you are, I'd guess you aren't very successful. The whole intimidating-trooper-in-uniform thing is sort of a turn-off." The wickedness in Quinton's eyes told him something else was coming. "Now, Wyatt in his uniform is a whole different matter." He grinned, and Mark remained stone-faced.

"I'm serious," Mark said.

"So am I. If you want to know about our relationship, then ask Wyatt, and he can decide what he wants to tell you. I'm not going to spin tales out of school, and I don't kiss and tell. What's between him and me is private, and he can decide what he wants you to know. As for the real situation at hand, I promise I'll tell you if I find out anything else, but right now, you both know all I know."

Mark's expression softened like he had gotten something he wanted.

"You can sit down if you like. I need to get Callum a bottle before he blows." He left the room.

"Was that really necessary?" Wyatt asked softly.

Mark nodded. "I had to know if he was serious or just playing some kind of game. I think the guy is serious, and I agree with you. He's just as confused by what's happened as anyone."

"Okay. So can you stop the dick routine now?" Wyatt hated Quinton being put on the spot.

"Maybe." He sat on the edge of one of the chairs. "I think Quinton doesn't know, but I also have to wonder if some of the people around him aren't as pure as the driven snow."

Quinton returned, and Mark turned to him. "Would you be willing to give us the names of the people you believe were at that party? It may be the start of some of this."

Quinton sat down with Callum in his arms and gave him the bottle. "And you'll contact all my friends, and then what? I'll have a bunch of pissed-off people in my life. Not that I intend to hang out with them, but I don't want them to hate me either."

"Give me the list, and Mark and I will check them out. We won't talk to them unless we have a reason to. But it's likely someone close to you did this, and if we find out who it is, we may get the answers we both need." He smiled, hoping that Quinton would trust him.

"Okay." He stood and passed Callum into Wyatt's arms. Wyatt happily took over feeding and sharing smiles while Quinton got a pad and began to write. "You promise you won't be showing up on their doorstep and saying that I gave you their names?" He continued working. "A lot of these guys are people I grew up with who helped me get through some rough times. They're suspicious enough of the police." He finished and handed the page to Mark before taking Callum back. "I don't think any of these guys are going to help."

"Do you know if Jennifer is seeing anyone?" Mark asked again.

"You already asked. It isn't like she and I are on speaking terms right now. Maybe you could ask her. Now, she's someone I wouldn't mind you paying a visit to. Heck, talk to her all you like. Take her to the station. She's out on bail after all because charges are still pending. And she has the most to gain from a stunt like that." Quinton took over feeding Callum once again, and after a few seconds, he pulled the bottle away and gently burped Callum before resuming feeding, but he seemed done and awake, huge blue eyes taking in everything.

"We'll do our best," Mark said before standing. "You weren't at all how I expected."

"Oh?" Quinton asked.

"Yeah." Then Mark actually smiled. "Thank you for your help." Mark left, and Wyatt followed him outside.

"What was that about?" Wyatt demanded as soon as the door closed.

Mark walked to the car and slid into the driver's seat. Wyatt climbed in as well. "I figured he'd be a weaselly guy, but he isn't. He stood up for himself and stayed factual. I didn't get any sense that he was lying to us." Mark tapped the steering wheel to some inaudible beat in his head. "I get the sense that he's as genuine as he seems to be, which sucks, because it makes me look like a real douche. But I had to know if he was part of this."

Wyatt was relieved, and yet he wanted to smack Mark on the back of the head. Of course he wasn't part of it—Wyatt had known that already. It was impossible for him to have been. But he was pleased Mark thought so too.

"I really want to talk to this Jennifer."

"Me too. There was a tip that was conveniently called in about the drugs, and Kip Rogers played it for Quinton, but he didn't recognize the voice. That doesn't really mean anything. There are lots of ways to disguise that through a computer, so it's really difficult to say who might be behind it. My money is still on Jennifer… somehow."

"We'll get to the bottom of it," Mark said and started the car. "Let's check and see if we have any new information."

Wyatt knew that sometimes a case took legwork and sheer determination, but he wondered how many obstacles they would have to face before they made real progress.

# CHAPTER 10

"The hearing is in a few days, and Donald is jittery because of the drugs that were planted. He says it's not that he doesn't believe me, but he's getting pressure from his supervisors because they say that he should have been cautious and removed Callum," Quinton told Wyatt, his voice shaking. He held Callum for his own comfort. "What am I going to do? Will the judge feel the same way and put him in foster care just because they were here? They weren't mine. You believe that, and so do the police." It seemed like his life was imploding around him, and there was nothing he could do to stop it.

"Mark and I are going to interview Jennifer tomorrow, and we're going to do it at the station. Since she's out on bail, we have every right to question her, and even the captain agrees that she could be a link." Wyatt sat down. "Trust that we're doing the best we can. I can't say much more about an ongoing investigation, but we are working hard. It really seems like the drugs placed here are linked to our larger investigation, though so far I haven't figured out how. But the answers are out there, and we'll find them." Wyatt sounded so confident.

Quinton wanted to believe him, but the shadow of the upcoming hearing and the possibility of losing Callum eclipsed everything else. "What can I do?"

Wyatt sighed. "I have an idea, but I'm not sure you'll like it. Do your friends know that you're seeing me?"

Quinton nodded. "I'm sure they do. I talked to David about you, and he knows you're a trooper. Why?" He laid Callum on the floor so he could play with his activity set.

"Invite him over and I'll just happen to show up. I'd like to meet him. I know he'll be on his guard, but it might tell us something. He might have the answers to some of our questions and let them slip either to me or to you. I don't know. It's worth a try."

Quinton didn't know if it would do any good, but he figured it couldn't hurt. At the very least, some of the guys would get to meet Wyatt, and maybe they would realize he was a pretty good guy. "I can try." He figured now was as good a time as any and called David.

"Hey," David said when he answered, with enough overlapping voices behind him to make it a little hard to hear. "What's up?"

"I was just wondering if you wanted to come over for pizza and stuff." God, this was harder than he thought it would be. "But it sounds like you're busy."

The noise seemed to grow softer and then cut off, probably as David stepped outside. "I was just out for a drink with Steven, and we were going to get some dinner. I can order a few pizzas, and we could stop by after picking them up if you like. Is Callum going to be asleep, or will we be able to talk and stuff?"

"He's awake and playing right now. Hopefully he'll be up for a couple hours." Quinton met Wyatt's gaze and nodded. "I'm looking forward to seeing you guys." He hung up. "Okay, both he and Steven are going to come over with pizza. Why don't you go, and

I'll text quick when they arrive. You can show up fifteen minutes or so later. Be sure to wear really casual clothes and bring a pizza of your own." He needed Wyatt to seem like he had just popped by.

"I'm on my way." Wyatt gave Callum a tickle on the belly. God, Quinton hoped Wyatt could pull this off and that this little exercise didn't blow up in his face. Wyatt paused and leaned over the chair, intense eyes boring into Quinton. "Trust me," Wyatt whispered before kissing him. Quinton's eyes drifted shut, and Wyatt deepened the kiss, pressing harder, adding intensity before pulling away. "I'll see you in a little while."

Quinton nodded, wondering how Wyatt could short-circuit his brain in a matter of seconds. "Okay." He swallowed hard.

"Just be yourself while they're here. These guys are your friends, and you don't need to do anything. Maybe you can encourage them to gossip some, especially when I'm out of the room. Just pay attention to how they act and what they say." Wyatt kissed him again and then left the house.

Quinton wondered how he was going to keep his nerves from getting the better of him, but he knew Wyatt was right. First thing, it would be good for Wyatt to meet some of the other people in his life, and the rest of it was up to him. David already knew about Wyatt, so there should be no big reveal there. And if David knew, then so did Steven and everyone else in his old circle. David loved to talk, and maybe that could help them. All Quinton wanted was to find out who had broken into his house and planted the pot. If he had that information, it would change the dynamic of the upcoming hearing—something he desperately needed.

Callum whimpered, and Quinton straightened the rabbit from where Callum had hooked it around the top of the activity set. "You're getting strong, aren't you?" He released it, and Callum began playing with the bunny once again. He kicked and batted happily, but all Quinton seemed to be able to see right now was the moment that all this came crashing to an end and someone took his child away. He hated that he only seemed to be able to visualize the worst, but his fear had the better of him, and he had little doubt that it was only going to get harder.

QUINTON JUMPED at the knock on the door. Callum was half asleep from playing with his toys, and he fussed at the pounding noise. "It's okay. It's just company." He lifted him up and carried Callum to the door, soothing him. He opened it to David and Steven, who were carrying beer and pizza. The scent of it wrapped around him almost immediately.

"Come on in," he said with a smile.

"The little stinker is still up," David said, barely paying attention to Callum, while Steven paused to give his son a smile.

"Hi, little fella."

Callum chose that moment to be shy.

"Go ahead and have a seat. I need to give him a bottle, and then he'll go right down." It was dinnertime, so maybe Callum would sleep for a while. It was worth a shot. After warming one of the bottles he'd already made up, Quinton messaged Wyatt. Then he sat in his favorite chair with Callum.

"Dang, he's, like, tiny," Steven said, throwing open the lid on one of the boxes. He passed over a beer, but

Quinton declined it in favor of the soda he'd grabbed. "How much longer are you going to have him?"

Quinton shrugged. "It depends on the hearing, I guess."

"I never pictured you with a baby. I knew you and Jennifer had one, but still. It's hard to see you as Mr. Mom." He took a huge bite of pizza. "You know Jennifer is super mad at you. She was talking smack just the other day." He sat back.

"There's nothing I can do about her or what she did. She's the one who's going to need to answer for it." Quinton shifted Callum to burp him. "I heard Caleb took the car as a joke or something, but there's nothing I can do about it. The local police, Child Services, state police—they're all involved. I've had social workers and a bunch of other people all looking at what happened."

"She doesn't see it that way," Steven said.

Quinton was just about to argue with him, but he held his tongue and calmed himself before speaking. "I'm not the bad guy here. I saw the car being taken and raced after it. My God, he was doing nearly a hundred on the freeway. Callum could have been killed. I know both Jennifer and Caleb are in trouble, but it has nothing to do with me."

He gave Callum the rest of his bottle, burped him again, and put him to bed just before Wyatt knocked on the door.

"Hey, come on in. I wasn't expecting you. I've got some friends here." He hoped he wasn't overacting.

"Hey, guys," Wyatt said as he entered the living room. "I guess great minds think alike." Wyatt turned to Quinton. "Sorry. I didn't mean to interrupt. I can just go and leave you guys alone." He went to leave.

"Nah, we were just talking," David said. "It's cool."

"Guys, this is Wyatt," Quinton said.

"The cop," Steven mumbled, and David bumped his shoulder. He sat up and finished his slice before grabbing another.

"He saved Callum when dipshit Caleb stole the car and nearly killed him." Quinton wasn't going to take any crap from them.

"Didn't he pull you over?" Steven asked grouchily.

"Yeah. But he listened to me when I told him about Callum, and he didn't give me a ticket." Quinton grinned, and even Steven smiled at that.

"What do you all do?" Wyatt asked as he snagged a slice and one of the beers he'd brought.

"I work in sales, and Steven is part owner of Group's Garage with his father," David explained. "He's really talented under the hood. So I've been told." He nudged Steven's arm, and Quinton rolled his eyes. It was an old joke. "Steven here is our ladies' man."

"Nice," Wyatt said.

"You better believe it." Steven grinned as he sat back. "You all can eat your heart out." Quinton snickered and then did it again. "What?"

"Don't say that to gay guys. They might think it's some kind of invitation." Quinton looked at David, who hooted and fist-bumped him. Steven groaned, and Wyatt laughed. David was straight, well mostly, as far as Quinton knew… and was secure in himself at any rate.

"That was really bad," Steven complained.

"So were you, bragging about bagging women in front of a gay guy. Not only do we not do that sort of thing, most of the women we know are like our sisters, so that's really yucky," Wyatt teased, and David went right along with it.

"Not our Quinton here," Steven interjected.

"One time. I was drunk and was with Jennifer *one time*." He turned to Wyatt. "You'd think I'd have to turn in my gay card or something." Quinton rolled his eyes, and Wyatt patted his leg. "It was one of the biggest mistakes I ever made, though I did get Callum out of it. But it wasn't fair to Jennifer." He sipped some more of his soda and finished his piece of pizza. You'd think he'd been drinking with how morose he felt.

"She was pretty pissed when it didn't work out. Apparently she'd had her eye on you for a while," David told him. "So when you two got together, she thought it would be smooth sailing after that."

Quinton leaned forward. "But I had told her I was gay."

The guys shrugged.

"Sometimes people believe what they want to believe is true, and no amount of facts will dissuade them," Wyatt said softly.

"Jennifer is a really intense woman," Steven commented.

David sipped his beer and set the bottle on the coffee table, leaning forward. "Are you interested in her? I didn't think she was your type."

"What *is* your type?" Wyatt asked.

"Gullible," David teased.

"Asshole," Steven said without heat. "No. I like a girl with super long legs and eyes as big as anything. I also like my women a little less... demanding... if you know what I mean. Jennifer just isn't my type, but I hear she is Remmy's type." He grinned.

Wyatt excused himself to use the bathroom.

"He isn't bad for a cop. But I keep thinking he's listening to everything we say so he could use it against us," Steven said as soon as Wyatt was out of the room. "He seems nice enough, though, and he has a sense of humor."

"Who's Remmy?" Quinton asked.

"He's a guy who came to the last party at the house. Caleb brought him—said he was a guy he'd met and thought was cool."

"Where did Jennifer meet him?" Quinton tried not to sound too interested.

"She showed up Sunday afternoon knocking on the door, and they already seemed to know each other. Seemed kind of chummy. I got the feeling they had met before, and then the two of them sort of settled off by themselves. You know how couples are sometimes. I was a little out of it after Saturday night and still mellow, so we just left them alone, but they left together at some point." Steven went back to eating and drinking the last of his beer once Wyatt returned to the room. "It was a great party. Too bad you missed it."

"I had Callum. It really seems like my party days are pretty much over. Callum goes to bed about seven or eight, and he's up one or two times a night. Then I have to go to work, pick him up at day care, and go back through the routine all over again."

"Yeah, but what if Jennifer gets him back?" Steven asked, and Quinton wanted to slap him. "You know mothers usually get custody and all. She is his mother. So what will you do if the court gives him back?"

Quinton shrugged, but he knew he would be gutted like a caught salmon. There was no way around it. "How would you feel if your child was taken away?" he retorted, looking at each of them.

"If I had a kid, it would be his mother's responsibility to take care of him," Steven said, as serious as a heart attack.

David groaned. "You are such a pig. No wonder no one will stay with you for more than two weeks. I gave Quinton grief because I didn't understand, but Callum is his kid, and he takes this seriously. Did your dad stick around? Of course he didn't. Mine wasn't there much either."

Steven murmured something that might have been agreement.

"I'm just trying to give my kid a better chance than we had." Quinton's life boiled down to that. All he wanted was to be the best father he could be. "Is it really that hard to understand? My mother was a lot more like Jennifer than she was one of those television mothers, and I don't want Callum to have that kind of life. You don't have to agree with me, but it's my decision, and you should respect it."

Both David and Steven nodded slowly. "But we miss you," David said, and Steven glanced at Wyatt as though the changes in their lives were all his fault somehow.

"Things change. What do you think is going to happen when you find someone special?" Quinton asked David. "Or Steven, what if you decide you've found someone who makes you want to stop being a total man-slut and settle down? You might have kids of your own." Steven paled and seemed like he was going to be sick for a second. Clearly that idea hadn't crossed his mind. "You do know what causes such things to happen… right?"

"Fuck off," Steven groused. "I like my life."

"Good. But it will change. I guess I've learned that nothing stays the same no matter how hard we might wish it would."

"If the shoe were on the other foot, would you feel the same way you do now?" Wyatt asked, and color rose in Steven's cheeks. He lowered his gaze and finished his beer. That was all the answer Quinton needed.

"So to get this conversation on juicier topics, what do you know about Remmy?" Quinton asked. "If Jennifer *is* dating him, then Callum could come in contact with the guy." Getting people to talk about what you wanted them to was hard.

"Subtle," David said.

"Yeah… I knew you were worried about Jennifer," Steven said, and Quinton breathed an inward sigh of relief. He wasn't, but he'd let them think so.

"I don't know much about the guy."

"Hmmm." Quinton glanced at Wyatt. "What mind of name is Remmy anyway?"

"His real name is Raymond or something," David piped up. "He drove a fancy new car to the party, wore expensive clothes and jewelry. I thought he was trying to make a splash and impress everyone. You know the type."

Steven shrugged. "Didn't seem like that to me. He was totally comfortable, like he always had cash or something. I mean, the guy didn't even bring anything to contribute, not even a six-pack. Just showed up with Caleb and drank the entire time he was there. The guy's a wannabe. If he had all the cash he was trying to look like he sported, then he wouldn't have been so cheap." He leaned forward.

"Did you see his shoes?" David asked.

Steven rolled his eyes, and Quinton met Wyatt's gaze for a second. "You and your shoes." David did have this thing for shoes. He had hundreds of pairs going back years and never threw any of them out. The guy went to yard sales and secondhand stores looking for interesting shoes in his size. Quinton figured that everyone had their thing that made them happy, and there were worse things than shoes.

"He had on nice clothes, but fancy new shoes. Expensive ones." David shrugged and closed the lid on the empty pizza box, then reached for a slice from one of the others. "He seemed to make Jennifer happy, but there was something off about him. I don't know what it was. But he spent all his time with Jennifer and didn't mix with anyone else. That was kind of strange to me. Even when other people said hello, he barely stopped paying attention to her."

"Maybe the guy is really in love with her or something," Quinton offered.

Both David and Steven shook their heads.

"It wasn't that kind of attention. He wasn't all over her, and they weren't kissy-face. It was different and kind of weird."

"Conspiratorial," David offered. "Like they were up to something."

Callum began fussing in the other room, so Quinton went in to get him. "That was a short nap," he said softly and quickly realized why. "Somebody has a full diaper." He got him changed and cleaned up before getting a small bottle. Callum's eyes were already droopy when Quinton sat back down with the guys to give Callum a small amount of formula as his eyes closed.

"He is a cute little guy," David commented as he leaned over the chair to take a look. "Callum does look like you, I guess. I never really saw that in babies before. People always say that a baby looks like his mom or dad, but they're babies. They look like babies. My cousin had a baby a couple years ago. Ugliest thing I ever saw."

"David," Quinton chided. "Babies are not ugly."

"This one was. Oh my goodness. Though my cousin was never going to win any beauty contests."

"That's terrible. I've met your cousin, remember? She's kind of pretty. You're just being queenie, man, and it isn't attractive. People look the way they do. Lord knows you aren't going to win any hunkiest man contests." Not that he was either, but still. "What I want to know is when we all became a bunch of gossipy Gregs. We sit here eating pizza and telling stories about ugly babies and antisocial party guests. It's not like any of us is a major catch." He held their gazes. David shrugged, and Steven tried to puff his chest out and failed. "Wyatt is the exception. He's hunky."

"Yeah, yeah, rub it in," David sassed. He finished his pizza and tossed the bit of crust into the second empty box. There were only a few slices left in the last box, and Steven dove right in.

"I need to put Callum in bed." Quinton left once again and got Callum settled in his crib and took a second to watch him sleep.

"You really do look like a father," David whispered from the doorway. Quinton left the room, keeping the door open enough that he could hear if Callum woke. "I guess it's kind of strange to see one of your friends as a parent. We were kids together, and now you have a kid." He sounded like he was starting to understand.

Steven's phone rang, and he answered it with a groan. "Must be his mother," David whispered. "He only acts like that when she calls, and she always wants something."

"Okay. ... Okay," Steven said quietly. "I'll be right there. ... No, I'm at Quinton's. He has the baby, so we went there." He rolled his eyes dramatically. "Give me a few minutes." He hung up and stood. "I gotta go. There's some problem in my mom's bathroom, and I have to fix it." He patted Quinton on the shoulder and hurried out.

David helped Quinton gather up the trash and carry it out back.

"Wyatt seems nice enough," David said. "Doesn't say too much, though."

Quinton smiled. "I like him, and he seems to like me." He knew he sounded like a teenager. "We'll have to see what happens. The hearing for Callum is on Friday." He closed the lid on the trash can. "I'm nervous as hell."

"I know. Just be honest. Heck, you convinced Steven that being a father isn't the worst thing in the world or some kind of death sentence. If you can do that, the judge will be no problem at all." David hugged him and then walked through the house. Quinton heard David say goodbye to Wyatt before leaving.

He locked the back door and joined Wyatt.

"Your friends seem nice enough," Wyatt said.

"They're not bad guys. Just had a rough life like me." He sat down, finally able to relax. "I guess you have the same question as me. Who is Remmy? He seems chummy with Jennifer."

"I wanted to ask for a description, but I couldn't figure out how to work it into the conversation." Wyatt said.

"Wait." Quinton pulled out his phone, then groaned when it had died again. He plugged it in and waited for the annoying thing to power up. "I really need a new one." He went to his messages and began sending pictures to Wyatt, his phone chiming with each one. "David sent me some pictures from the party. I figured he was drunk-texting me and didn't pay a lot of attention." Once he'd sent them over, he let his phone charge and looked the pictures over with Wyatt.

"What am I looking at?" Wyatt asked.

"Okay. It looks like these are from that Saturday night. It's mostly the guys having a good time." He continued through the pictures. "The crazy things people do." He remembered when he used to do the exact same things. Heck, Steven was half naked, hanging on some poor girl, in one of the pictures. "He sent me these on Sunday."

Wyatt continued through. "Is that Jennifer?" He leaned closer as if making sure on the small screen.

"Yeah, and the guy we can see part of must be Remmy." There was only part of him, and it wasn't a good picture. "But he came with Caleb." Quinton went back and smiled. "That's the same guy standing next to Caleb. That has to be him. Does he seem familiar?"

"Not to me, but maybe he will to someone else." Wyatt hugged him tight and hard. "You did amazingly well. I knew you were worried a little, but they had no idea that you weren't having a normal conversation, and they told you plenty."

"Yeah. I was wondering about Jennifer and some new boyfriend. Do you think that she got Remmy to plant the stuff here in the house?"

Wyatt shrugged. "I don't know. But we've got a couple of leads." He stepped away to talk on the phone for a few minutes. "Okay, Mark. Let's check and see if our suspects recognize him. If they do, it's a step forward." He hung up and hugged Quinton again.

"They thought I was jealous when I was asking about Remmy and Jennifer." He almost chuckled, but he held back while Wyatt sent some messages.

"Sorry. I need to get these pictures to Mark." He seemed excited, but Quinton didn't know exactly why. He thought that Jennifer had probably enlisted Remmy's help to get the pot and break into the house to plant it, and maybe she had gotten him to make the phone call. Either way, if they could prove it, it would take a lot of the pressure off him.

"What do we do next?" Quinton asked. "Who do you want me to talk to? Should we talk to Jennifer and see if we can get anything out of her?" He just knew she was behind all this.

"You? Nothing. I don't want you to do anything other than take care of Callum and keep him safe. That's your primary job. I appreciate your help, but if you go poking your nose into this any further, your friends are going to get suspicious, and I don't want to mess things up for you if we're on the wrong track." He gently rubbed Quinton's back.

Quinton held on to Wyatt and tried not to let the worry that seemed so damned present all the time take over again. There had to be a way that they could prove once and for all who had placed the drugs in his house.

"But Wyatt, you know that no matter what anyone says, as long as this hangs over me, it's going to be harder for me to keep Callum. The judge is going to have to choose between the two of us, and if I'm not a perfect parent, they're going to return him to Jennifer or send him to foster care." He held on tighter, trying to figure out a way out of this. He wanted to scream.

"Come on. It's late enough, and you're tired as all hell." After checking on the baby, Wyatt helped Quinton undress, and he slipped into bed. When Wyatt turned out the lights, Quinton expected him to leave, but soon enough Wyatt climbed in after him, curling close, his arms around him, holding tight. "It's okay. We'll figure things out."

"I hope so." It was all he had to hold on to.

# CHAPTER 11

WYATT HATED to go to work. It was supposed to be his normal day off, but he couldn't let the investigation sit. There was plenty to do, and a lot of it required good old-fashioned legwork.

"Quinton," he said softly as Callum cooed to himself in his crib. He knew from experience that was only going to last so long, and then his lungs would take over and Callum would become quite insistent.

"Oh God. Is it morning already?" He pushed back the covers and blearily got out of the bed, his boxers just hanging on his hips. Quinton must have lost some weight, from the way they barely stayed in place. "Come on, Bubba, let's get you changed and have some breakfast." He got Callum out of the crib, and Wyatt used that time to go to the bathroom and dress. "Do you want something?" Quinton asked when he made it out of the bedroom. He was already feeding Callum. "What time is it?"

"A little after seven. I need to go in and check on things. Hopefully the lab will have something to go on this morning." He kissed Quinton and gently rubbed Callum's downy head. He really was the cutest baby… and his father was pretty high on the hotness scale. "I'll call you later." He hated to go, but maybe he'd have some answers that might advance his case and help Quinton at the same time. On his way out, he packed up a beer bottle that each of the guys had held the night before.

He stopped at home to change into his uniform before going to the station. He cleared his email and checked on the lab results. They had been able to get DNA from the cigarettes, but there wasn't currently a match. The lab also got fingerprints from the bag that was at Quinton's. They were not a match to Quinton, which was good. They also didn't match the fingerprints for Jennifer that were now in the system. However, they did find the prints of one of the suspects in custody on the bag, which told him exactly nothing other than to confirm where the drugs had been packed. It was the unidentified print that interested him.

He dusted the bottles and ran for a match but got nothing. At least that eliminated two of Quinton's friends.

"If you keep coming in this early, I'm going to think you've started sleeping here. We get anything?" Mark asked.

Wyatt brought him up to speed. "The man in the pictures we know as Remmy matches the description of the mystery man the suspects described."

"We can show one of them the picture and see what we get," Mark offered. "I'll take care of that while you figure out who we need to see in the area. Maybe there are people who have seen activity and didn't realize what it was." Mark had a point, but Wyatt knew it was unlikely. That part of the county was sparsely populated, which was why the distribution point was placed there. Still, people watched, and maybe they'd get lucky.

THEY DIDN'T. The folks living in the area had all thought that it was a homeless encampment and they'd stayed away, so that was no help. Wyatt spent most of the day at it but got no information whatsoever. He pulled into the station and sat in the cruiser for a few minutes, trying to rearrange the pieces in his head. It really seemed strange to be coming to the station like this. Normally he spent his days working out of his car, but with this assignment, he was spending more time in the office. Since his thoughts were getting him nowhere, he went inside, where the captain met him. "What's going on?"

"Mark is about to go in with the first suspect." He led Wyatt to the interrogation area, where they watched the happenings on a screen. The suspect didn't look much better than he had when Wyatt had spoken to him.

"Is he okay?"

The captain shook his head. "We've got him enrolled in a drug treatment program. He's coming off some pretty heavy stuff. They're trying to help him." The captain grew quiet while Mark asked his questions and passed over a set of images, including one that Quinton had sent Wyatt.

"That's the guy. He thought he was so much better than the rest of us." He pointed right at Remmy.

"You're sure?" Mark asked. The suspect nodded.

"He sat away from everybody else, smoking and doing very little work the entire time. If he was going to be there, he should have helped at least." He seemed indignant, which made him believable.

"Good work. Where did you get the picture?" Captain Harker asked.

Wyatt explained how the case had intersected with his personal life.

"Are you sure of your feelings on this?"

"Mark talked to Quinton, and even he's convinced that Quinton has nothing to do with this," Wyatt said. "Some friends sent him the pictures from the party, and it seems that Remmy is involved with Callum's mother. She was the one we took in for leaving her baby in an unattended vehicle." Wyatt rolled his eyes. "I know it sounds like a soap opera, but those images and the description of the guy his ex was seeing led to the pictures, which led us to an identification. Now we just need to get this Remmy's full name and we'll have something to go on."

"In the meantime, put out a BOLO with the best description we have. I want to get him in here. He may be the guy behind this, or the next link in the chain upward… and I want him." The captain's eyes were as hard as steel. "We're getting pressure to solve this case, and the longer it goes on, the more likely the people behind it are going to fold up and get out of Dodge. We've been able to keep things quiet after the initial discovery, but this has to come to closure soon."

"I understand." The longer the case was open, the less likely it was to be solved. The news was filled with old cases that got solved, but while those made headlines, they were very rare. The fact was that the longer a case hung open, the less likely it would be solved. "I'm on it." The captain left, and Mark ended the interview and joined Wyatt in the observation room.

"It's progress." He set down the pictures.

"Okay. Now we have to find him."

Mark grinned. "That's the easy part. We're going to have a talk with Jennifer. She knows him, and she can either cooperate or have her bail revoked. It's that simple." He was as stern as hell.

"Let's go. I have her address," Wyatt said, and they headed out. It was just before dinnertime, and Wyatt pushed his hunger aside as he wondered about Quinton. He might be close to getting some answers that would help him. That would be great. As he drove, he checked the time, realizing that Quinton would be picking up Callum about now. He smiled, and Mark shook his head from the passenger seat. "Jesus, you really need to get your head in the game. Whenever it's quiet, you smile and get all happy. You're thinking about Quinton and that kid, aren't you?"

Wyatt pulled his attention away from Quinton and onto the task at hand. "What's wrong with that?"

"Nothing, except your head isn't where it's supposed to be, and that can be dangerous. You can't let your attention wander. I've been doing this sort of thing for a while, and you never know what can happen. This isn't a routine traffic stop. This is speaking to a witness who is most likely going to be hostile." Mark squirmed in his seat. "You have good instincts, really good ones. You instantly made the connection between this case and what was happening with Quinton, and by furthering one, you pushed the other forward as well and made a valuable connection. But trust me. I know it's hard, but leave the personal life at home. Keep your head on the job, or you could lose it."

Wyatt knew Mark was right, but dammit, Quinton made him happy. He pushed those thoughts away as he pulled up in front of the current address they had for Jennifer Winters. It was a low brick ranch house that apparently belonged to a relative. Since her folks had put up the bail, they wanted her close to family. It seemed they didn't trust their daughter completely either.

Wyatt cleared his head of everything but the case and got out of the car. He squared his shoulders and rang the doorbell, with Mark behind and off to the side. "Good evening," Wyatt said once the door was answered, presumably by Jennifer's aunt… maybe?

"May we help you?"

"We'd like to speak with Jennifer," Wyatt said.

She lowered her gaze. "If this is about that party she went to, we aren't happy either, and we moved her in here so we could watch over her. I can assure you she will not be attending any others." She was forceful and determined. "We have her with us to ensure that she maintains the strictest adherence to her bail."

"This isn't about the party but one of her friends. We need to speak with her." Wyatt wondered what Jennifer's aunt thought she might have done.

"She was on the phone the last time I checked. Please come in and I'll get her." She turned away, almost regally, and went down the hall. Wyatt and Mark stood near the door. The home was warm, the walls filled with family pictures.

"What do you want?"

"Jennifer!" her aunt snapped. "Behave yourself. These men have some questions for you."

"Does this have to do with my case? Because my lawyer has told me not to speak to anyone."

"This is about another matter, though if you like, we can take you down to the station and you can call your lawyer," Mark said flatly. "That is fully within your rights."

She looked to her aunt, who nodded. "What do you want to know?"

Mark pulled out one of the photographs of Remmy and handed it to her. "Do you know him?" Mark

seemed cold. "And before you answer, we have photographs of you at a certain gathering with him. Social
media can yield a wealth of information." Damn, Mark
was clever with how he covered their tracks. He never
said that was where they got the pictures, but it left that
impression. "I'll ask again. Do you know him?"

Her deep brown eyes filled with suspicion and fear.
She was seconds from lying but seemed to change her
mind. "Yeah, I know him. Name's Remmy."

"In the pictures we saw, you were pretty chummy
with him. Do you know his last name?" Mark stepped
closer, towering over her. Wyatt stepped back and let
him take the lead. He seemed to be a master at getting
information from people.

"Remington. That's why they call him Remmy.
His first name is Raymond, but he hates it. I mean, Ray-
mond Remington. What were his parents thinking?"
She rolled her eyes. "Is there anything else?"

Mark crossed his arms over his chest. "I'll remind
you that one of the conditions of your bail is that you
do not consort or have contact with anyone engaging in
or having been convicted of a crime. Drug offenses are
considered a crime. A phone call to your 'friend' Remmy would be considered contact, and your bail would
be revoked instantly. In that case, you would return to
jail, where you would remain until your trial is con-
cluded. Am I making myself clear?"

Jennifer nodded, but her aunt was something else.
"Go get your phone and give it to me. We used our sav-
ings to bail you out of jail, and we will not put that in
jeopardy." She held out her hand. Jennifer glared mur-
derously at Mark but handed it over to her aunt before
storming out of the room.

"Can I ask you men something?" Jennifer's aunt asked. "Have you seen my nephew? I know what Jennifer is accused of and that Callum has been removed from her care and he's with the father." Wyatt made no bid to confirm or deny. "Is Callum okay?"

Wyatt wanted to answer that he had held her nephew and that he and the father were both doing well. That they were amazing and already had a place in his heart. But he said nothing at all.

Mark's expression didn't change, and Wyatt wondered if he was going to say anything to her. Finally his expression softened slightly. "I've seen Callum, and he's a happy, healthy baby who, from what I can tell, is being well cared for and is genuinely loved. There is no doubt about that."

"I see." She bit her lower lip. "Do you think it might be possible for us to see him?"

"Contact Child Services. Callum is in their placement, and they would need to make that determination. But that's where you can start. Trooper Nelson is a friend of Callum's father, and he has seen Callum as well. If you follow the proper procedures, it should be possible for you to see your nephew." Mark smiled slightly. "Thank you for your help. We'll see ourselves out."

As soon as the door closed behind them, Wyatt breathed a sigh of relief. They didn't speak, though, until they were in the cruiser. "Now we have a name," Wyatt said, already putting it into the system. They got an address almost immediately, and Mark took off toward it, only to find the hollow shell of a burned-out home that had been that way long enough to have been boarded up and condemned. "Shit. Of course it couldn't be that easy."

"Things rarely are, though we sometimes get lucky. Check for previous addresses. I have a hunch," Mark said.

"Clue me in," Wyatt asked as he checked the system.

"It's simple. Say you're involved in some shady, even criminal enterprises, and from the kinds of drugs we recovered in that trailer, those involved are deep into it. You'd go through the process of having your address changed to throw anyone who might be looking off the scent. It's easy enough to do, especially if you have a color printer and a few computer skills."

"I got it, and it's on West South Street. Let's head on over and see if we get lucky." Meanwhile, Wyatt updated the BOLO with the information they had gathered so far. It was progress, and Wyatt could taste them wrapping up this case. That would be a real feather in his cap.

Mark drove, and Wyatt watched out the windows for any sort of suspicious activity. Using the address, he checked to see who owned the property they were headed to and smiled. "It seems to be a grandmother, based on her birthdate and the same last name." So maybe they were getting close.

Not to be. When they knocked on the door, it was answered by a middle-aged lady in light purple scrubs. "Can I help you? I'm Mrs. Remington's nurse. She requires permanent care."

"I see. Is Raymond ever here?"

"I've been working here for six months and he came once, a few days ago. Otherwise there's just a daughter who comes to see her. Mrs. Remington doesn't get visitors, which is a shame. She's a really nice lady." She invited them inside, but they demurred and headed back to their car. "Gentlemen!" she called as she stepped back out of the house. "He brought part of a pizza, and there was this delivery slip on the box." She passed it over, and Wyatt thanked her before she went back inside.

Wyatt checked the addresses he had on file with the one on the slip.

"Is it a new one?"

"Yeah. And it's out of town, closer to our crime scene." He sat back as Mark headed west. He followed the GPS and turned onto a residential country street with modest ranch homes on large lots. "That's it right there." It was easy to pick out because it was still broad daylight, every curtain was pulled, and the house had this hunkered-down feeling. The grass needed cutting, and the roof was covered in debris, with lichen growing in the shade of a half-dead tree.

"Do you want to stop?"

Wyatt shook his head. "Not right now. Just go on past and we'll circle around. I don't want to alarm the guy if he's watching, and I'm pretty sure he is," Wyatt said as they glided right on by without slowing down.

"Let's call this in, get a warrant, and come back with reinforcements," Mark suggested. He turned around in a driveway and headed back up the street. Ahead, the garage door slid open and a classic Dodge muscle car pulled out and made a turn ahead of them. Wyatt ran the plate. "That's him." He called in the make and model. "Suspect is heading west on Ritner Highway." As soon as the blue muscle car made the corner, it sped up, and the trees obscured the view. Mark reached the corner just in time for them to see the other car zooming away at near top speed.

Their lights flashed and sirens blared as they sped after him, Mark concentrating on the road, Wyatt relaying their position to anyone available. They were only going to get one shot at this. If Remmy got away, it was likely he wasn't going to be coming back for anything. This was a flight for his life and his freedom. Wyatt knew it in his gut.

Other units responded that they were up ahead just as the suspect made a left, probably heading for the freeway. Wyatt held on as they went over a rise, the damned car nearly airborne, but he barely felt it. All that kept running through his mind was they needed to catch this man for the sake of the case... and for Quinton and Callum. If they were truly chasing Remmy, then it was possible that he had answers, not just about the drug distribution but regarding the placement of drugs at Quinton's.

"He's turning too fast," Wyatt said. Part of him hoped he'd be out of commission. But the fleeing driver managed to retain control of the car, and it zoomed off. Wyatt held the oh-shit handle as Mark took the corner and sped after him. He updated dispatch on their location as the driver made another turn up ahead. This one was narrow, and Mark had to slow way down to make it.

"Shit!" Mark swore, and so did Wyatt. The road ahead was clear. They continued forward, checking down side streets in a small country residential settlement.

"We lost him." Wyatt clenched his fists and checked behind them just as the car passed the end of the road on its way out. "Turn around."

"Crap," Mark said. He whipped into a driveway and then backed out and peeled off back the way they'd come. Wyatt stayed on the radio, giving updates as they went back to the main road. They saw nothing in either direction. The other car had vanished. Wyatt groaned and wanted to beat the crap out of something. Other units were in the area, but none of them spotted the car, and Wyatt knew there was nothing they could do at the moment. A wide-net call with a description of the car was put out for the area, but they were forced to give up. "Let's get a warrant and see if we can learn anything from the house."

It was only a consolation prize. Maybe they would learn something useful, but they had lost the man himself. Now it was fucked up, and Wyatt had no idea if he'd get this close to Remmy again. If it were Wyatt, he'd be on his way to the other side the country with no intention to return.

# CHAPTER 12

"HE GOT away," Wyatt told Quinton when he stopped by after work. Quinton was happy to see him, but wished Wyatt had better news. "We found where he was staying and went through the house. The place was a mess, with dishes and trash everywhere. Remmy is most definitely a complete slob, but surprisingly there was very little of a personal nature in the house."

"Is it his place?" Quinton felt the dark shroud of reality washing over him.

"He told the neighbors he was house-sitting. The owners have been taking care of their daughter in California for the past couple months, and he simply moved in. Those poor people are going to have one hell of a shock when they get home. It seems he'd been just hiding there."

"Where does it leave us? Can you catch him anyway?" Quinton asked.

"We're going to try. We have some leads to follow up, and we're going back to talk to people we've already seen to make sure we haven't missed anything. This is the difficult part in any investigation. There will be setbacks, but we aren't going to give up. Somehow we will figure out what's going on." Wyatt sounded so definite. "But the one bit of good news is that we were able to tie Remmy's fingerprint to one on the bag of drugs we found here. That says that he handled it. We also found one of our other suspects' prints on it."

Quinton shrugged. "So? That only means that they both handled it."

Wyatt shook his head. "Remmy's prints overlapped one of the others, which means he touched it afterward. So it's likely he was the one to plant the drugs, and if he is, then there's one person who may be able to help us." He kept pacing back and forth in the small room like a caged lion.

"Jennifer," Quinton said softly, lightly holding an awake and alert Callum on his lap. "How do we get it out of her? She isn't just going to tell you or Mark that she asked Remmy to plant the drugs for her."

Wyatt seemed to ponder that for a while. "No. Maybe she won't tell us, but she might tell you." Some idea was cooking in Wyatt's mind; Quinton could see it in his eyes. "Let me think on this."

"Okay. But two heads are better than one," Quinton said.

"Yeah, I know." Wyatt finally settled on the sofa next to him. "But it's just a notion." He rested his head against Quinton's shoulder. "Let me think about it." He sighed, and Quinton sat still.

"Can I ask you something else?" Quinton asked. "We're supposed to go to your parents' for dinner, and…." He swallowed. "What are we going to tell them? I mean, we haven't talked about it. I know your mom is interested in meeting Callum and me, but I don't know what to tell them when I see them." God, he couldn't seem to put together a decent coherent thought. He'd been wondering all day what to say or how to ask.

"Are you trying to ask if you're my boyfriend?" Wyatt smiled, and Quinton nodded. He hadn't been sure what Wyatt might consider him, and he hadn't wanted to push. "Because that's how I think of you."

"Oh good," Quinton said, and Wyatt turned slightly so he could look into Quinton's eyes. They moved to each other without saying anything more. Just as Wyatt's lips touched Quinton's, Callum began to laugh and bounce. Wyatt deepened the kiss and then pulled away and grinned at Callum. "It seems he approves too."

"Yeah, I guess he does." Wyatt seemed far away for a few seconds. "Sorry. I keep wondering what I'm going to do next. Usually things happen and we solve cases, but they don't come this close to home. I always want justice to be done and for the right things to happen."

"I know. It's just a few more days until the hearing. I got a call today from the social worker who was here to look over the house. Jennifer and her aunt have asked if they could visit with Callum before the hearing, and I told them it was okay." He wasn't going to be a dick about it. Heck, he hoped working with them would show that he wanted Callum to have a relationship with his mother, no matter what the outcome of the hearing... and eventual custody battle.

"When will they see him?" Wyatt asked as he tickled Callum, earning a smile and maybe a giggle.

"I agreed to tomorrow after work. They said I could take him to the visitation center if we wanted, but instead the social worker is going to meet us all at Letort Park. I can show Callum the ducks and their babies, and it will be good to get him outside for a while. She thought it a good idea too—less formal of a setting."

Wyatt nodded, and that faraway expression was back. "I'm thinking that while you're there and Jennifer's aunt is spending time with Callum, you might

want to talk to Jennifer. She has to think that she's created a lot of trouble for you, so let's see if she'll gloat
about it, even a little."

Quinton snorted. "I wish I had thought of that. Jennifer loves to get one over on other people. There is
nothing that makes her happier than being able to lord
it over someone or let them know that she got the better
of them somehow." All he needed to do was get her into
a position where she thought they were alone, and if he
approached her the right way, the temptation would be
too overwhelming.

"Yeah. But it has to be just the two of you, and I
don't know if the social worker will allow it."

"She might if she thinks that Jennifer and I are interested in deescalating the tension between us. That's
what she's going to want—a way for the two of us to
come to some agreement that we can both live with. Of
course I'm not going to believe a single word she says
about what she wants or any promises she makes, but if
I can get her to admit anything…." He swallowed hard.
"I don't know if I can do it, though."

"If you fail, then you haven't lost anything. However, if she does admit something, then there's the
chance that Mark and I can get a break and you might
get the information you need to show her for what she
is."

"I can try," Quinton said. "I'm not very good at
this, and Jennifer is pretty adept at pushing my buttons."

"Let her think she's getting the better of you. She'll
let her guard down, and maybe there will be something
you can use against her. After all, she is the one who
left Callum in the back seat of a car unattended because
he was fussy." A hint of anger colored Wyatt's voice.
"What the hell was she thinking? Callum isn't any

trouble." He leaned closer and softened his tone. "Are you? You're a good boy, and she's a terrible mother."

"You won't get any argument there," Quinton agreed. "Like I said, I'll give it a try. But what good is it if she tells me things? She can just deny them later, which is what she tries to do all the time. Then I'll look like an idiot." He hated that she had been able to do that to him.

"Whatever she says, you just report it to me, and I can try to find a way to prove it. We don't need to use her words against her directly. Just let her give us places that we can look. If we find the people who placed the drugs, I bet we find the people I'm after as well. The two events seem linked." From what Wyatt had told him, Quinton figured he was right.

"Okay." All he could do was try.

Callum began to fuss a little, and Quinton got him a bottle. Once he had fed him, he got him set up with some toys to keep him occupied for a while. "Can we talk about something else?" He'd had a hard day, with multiple people making demands on him. Quinton was exhausted, and thinking about the hearing on Friday only added anxiety to the issue.

"Of course. We could talk about my day, but I don't think it was any better than yours." Wyatt relayed some of what had happened, and Quinton was as disappointed as Wyatt seemed to be when Remmy got away. "We did confirm that he was staying in the house, though, and that he was the man in the pictures and working at the distribution site. So at least that part of the picture is pretty clear. He was also working for someone. He left a cell phone behind, and we were able to crack the security code to get into it. We have the phone number that is sending him the instructions, but nothing more than that. It's another step in the ladder, but we don't know how high it is or if we're even beginning to see the top of the thing."

"I wish I could help." Quinton covered his mouth as a yawn overtook him.

"There's nothing you can do with that part of the investigation."

Quinton let Callum play and leaned back, closing his eyes. What he needed was rest and a chance to relax, but he wasn't going to get it. Callum would need to be fed soon, and maybe he'd go down to sleep for a few hours before his little belly was ready for food again.

"Are you okay?"

Quinton blinked. "Yeah. Just worked out. Some of these days just take so much energy." He bent down and lifted Callum onto his lap. He was so active at the moment that Quinton wasn't sure what to do.

Wyatt lifted him off his lap. "Go on and lie down. I'll play with him." The two of them were already making goo-goo faces at each other.

Quinton didn't have the energy to argue and was simply grateful that Wyatt cared enough to give him a break. "I'll just be a few minutes," he said. He left the door open as he went into the bedroom and then lay on the bed, pulling a blanket over his legs.


"QUINTON," A soft voice said, pulling him put of sweet oblivion. He blinked in the dark room and remembered where he was.

"Shit…." He'd fallen asleep and forgotten his baby and everything. "Where's Callum?"

"In the bouncy thing your sister sent. He's perfectly happy and is probably going to need his bottle before he goes to bed," Wyatt told him gently. Then he leaned down and kissed him. "Nothing for you to worry about."

"How long have I been asleep?" He sat up, still blinking himself awake.

"A couple of hours. You really needed it. I have dinner in the kitchen, so why don't you get up and have a little to eat?"

"How did you do all this?" Quinton croaked, his throat dry.

"I didn't, any more than you can. Come on out and you can meet my mother. She called a while ago, and when I told her where I was, she came over and made dinner."

Quinton groaned. "Your mother is here? I look like crap, and the house is a mess, and…." He was shocked.

"Please. It's baby mess, and Mom has seen enough of that. Besides, she actually cooked dinner for us." He smiled. "It's really good. She made her glazed chicken with rice and vegetables. This stuff is worth walking five miles in the rain for. If you want, I'll tell her that you'll be out in a few minutes, but don't worry about it. Okay?" He hugged him. "Mom is already in love with your son."

"I just wanted to make a good impression."

Wyatt snickered. "You already have. She knows how hard it is to raise a baby, and she had Dad to help her. Believe me, you have nothing but her respect." Wyatt took his hand, and Quinton stood and let himself be led through his own home to the kitchen, where the table had been set with his best mismatched dishes and the room smelled like heaven.

"I'm sorry, Mrs. Nelson. Wyatt didn't tell me that you were here, and…." He stifled an errant yawn.

"Sweetheart, call me Lily, and don't you dare. I know how hard it is to raise a baby. Sleep is precious, and when I called and Wyatt said where he was, well, I sort of invited myself over and took over your kitchen. Wyatt can cook, but with all that's been going on, I'm sure the pizza place is on speed dial and that he's been a regular visitor at the drive-through." She met Wyatt's gaze, and Quinton snickered.

"I don't know about that, but he did cook for me. And I understand I have you to thank for the lovely picnic food." She was nice and seemed genuine. "Wyatt said you helped with that. Things came up, though, and we ended up eating it on the living room floor."

"There's always something that will come up with a baby," Lily said as she brought the plate of chicken to the table.

"Mom, if I remember right, it was my work that came up," Wyatt corrected.

She shrugged. "You know how I feel about your job. I understand that you love law enforcement, but I worry all the time." Wyatt sighed, and Quinton liked her even more. "There's so much going on." He could almost hear her stop herself before she reminisced about how things were in her day. A bowl of rice and some roasted vegetables were added to the table, and Quinton's appetite kicked in. His daily lunch of a sandwich and chips had been too long ago, and this smelled so amazing.

Wyatt sat as well, and his mother joined them. "Where did you two meet?" Lily asked. "Wyatt never said."

"He pulled me over on the freeway. I was chasing a stolen car with Callum in the back seat," Quinton said. "That was the most terrified I have ever been in my life.

Wyatt helped get the car stopped and returned Callum to me. Then we met again in parenting class, and he helped look after Callum while I was there." He smiled. "Then he asked me out after class, and I think I was hooked." He almost sighed like a high-schooler.

"Mom, let's just say that things have been a little out of the ordinary," Wyatt told her. "I don't think there are many people who met their boyfriend at a high-speed traffic stop."

"I don't suppose so. Why was Callum in the back seat?" She took a small bite.

"His mother, Jennifer, left him alone in the car because she got him to sleep and didn't want to wake him. She said she was just next door, leaving him unattended in the car." He tried to keep the scorn out of his voice and failed. "I'm challenging her for custody, and we have our first court appearance Friday." He wasn't sure it was possible to get any more nervous. "Wyatt has been helping me out, and so has Child Services. They arranged for day care so I can still work."

"Is having a baby something you always wanted?" Lily asked.

Quinton hesitated and then shrugged. "Things with Jennifer were a total mistake. I was trying to be something that I'm not. Then I found out she was pregnant and that I was the father. I refused to marry her, even though she was pressuring me to. But I was there for Callum, and I got a good job and paid the child support because it was for my son." He sighed. "I honestly expected to be an every-other-weekend dad." He took a few more bites and wondered why it was so easy to open up to Wyatt's mom.

"Then everything changed?" Lily offered, and Quinton nodded. "You saw Callum being taken away."

"Yeah, and all I could think was that I was never going to see him again. At the time, I had no idea why Jennifer would leave him in the car, but I saw it being taken and Callum through the back window. I didn't think of calling the police. All I knew was that I had to get him back, and I took off after the kidnapper." The turmoil and fear of that day rushed back at him in a huge way. "All I could think was, what if something happened to him?" He took Wyatt's hand. "Wyatt believed me after he pulled me over, and he helped save Callum."

"I take it you aren't used to being believed. Why?" She narrowed her eyes, and Quinton had a pretty good idea that Lily had heard things about him. Maybe that was why she'd come over.

"Because I did enough stupid stuff—too much of it as a kid. Wyatt has seen it all, if that's what you're worried about. I haven't held back stuff about my past with him." He could see the concern in Lily's eyes. "He deserves to know it all, and he's met some of my friends."

"How did that work out?" Lily asked as if she knew. Quinton was already wondering if she was psychic or something.

"They're suspicious of him, and I can't blame them. They were my support system growing up. My mother was pretty absent and into herself. She has her problems. So I spent a lot of time with my friends. They had my back, and I had theirs. That led me into things I regret now, but at the time we were all trying to survive. I didn't have someone like you or your husband to rescue me the way you took in Wyatt. I had to figure it all out on my own." He sighed.

"His friends are only just coming around to him wanting to be a parent," Wyatt interjected. "Some still seem to think that he should just let the mother take care of him and go back to his life the way it was."

Lily set down her fork. "Is that what you want to do? Parenthood is a huge responsibility, and you have the chance to step away from it if you really want." Her voice was soft, but the edge in the words raised Quinton's defenses.

"Is that what you did?" Quinton asked, not waiting for an answer. "I don't think so." He turned to Wyatt. "I don't get it. Do people think I'm completely useless? Everyone says the same thing. That I could just walk away as though Callum were nothing. Let someone else raise him. Hell, give him back to his mother so she can leave him in the car because he gets fussy for her and she finally got him to sleep. Let someone take him or... God knows what." His frustration was getting the best of him. "My friends don't get that I'm Callum's father and I can't just walk away from him. I won't. I'm going to fight for him. I may have to raise Callum alone, but I'm going to do a damn better job of it than my mother did." He turned to Lily, his gaze boring right through her, he was so angry. "What right does anyone have, thinking they can come into my home and talk like they know better than me what's best for Callum?"

Quinton took a deep breath and pushed back his chair. He went to where Callum sat in the bouncy chair and lifted him into his arms. Then he walked out of the room and took Callum to the bedroom. He needed the chance to hold him and just have a few minutes with his son. "I promise I'll always do my best for you. Okay? I may not be perfect, but I'll try." Callum blinked at him, and Quinton put Callum on his shoulder, gently rubbing his back, loving the warmth that radiated off him.

The bedroom door cracked open. He expected to see Wyatt, so he was surprised when Lily poked her head in. "I didn't mean to come off as the wicked parenting witch," she said, and it was impossible for Quinton to not smile.

"It wouldn't be so bad if I didn't wonder about those same things myself… all the time," he admitted. "What if I'm not good enough for him?" The raw emotion had largely evaporated, leaving behind the worry.

Lily chuckled lightly. "Sweetie, every parent feels the exact same way you do. At least every good parent that I know. When Randy was born, I was so scared. And when he got older, I kept telling my mother that I was afraid that I was going to mess up Randy because I couldn't have more kids and I didn't want him to grow up alone. I worried all the time."

"Well, I may not get to keep him after all. The initial hearing is Friday, and…." He shrugged. "Usually the state tries to return children, especially babies, to the mother, so I'll have to see what happens. But everyone who questions whether I can be a father may just get their wish after all." He held his head high. "No matter what, I'm not going to stop fighting for Callum. He deserves to be fought for." He took a deep breath and held Lily's gaze. She was all nice on the outside, but there was definitely a rod of steel underneath, and for some reason it seemed important to Quinton that she understand. Maybe it was because she was a good parent, and he didn't have many of those in his life.

"Mom," Wyatt said from the doorway, "let's ease up on the third degree so we can all have a nice dinner. All right?" The edge in his voice was hard to miss.

Quinton agreed and carried Callum back to his chair in the kitchen. Then he sat back down. "I get the feeling that was some kind of test."

"Yes," Wyatt agreed. "And it wasn't a very good one. Mom tends to be overprotective sometimes. Poor Randy got the treatment the first time he brought home a girl, and I swore the poor thing was two seconds from fainting."

"Forgive me. It's a mother's instinct, and I'm afraid I may have listened to some people who were spreading a little gossip," she admitted.

Quinton wished that wasn't true, but there was nothing he could do about it. His past was what it was, and while he was trying to move on from it, there were going to be people who would try to use it against him.

They settled down to a nice dinner with lighter conversation, thank God. Lily seemed much happier and less intense. The chicken was just as good as Wyatt had said it was, and Quinton ate plenty. Callum began fussing as he was finishing, and Quinton put him on his lap. He settled right away, happy that he could see what was going on.

"So, Lily, what is it you do?"

"I've sold real estate for more than twenty years. It started off as a hobby to make some extra money once the boys were in school. I was good at it, and eventually it grew into a full-time business. I really like it. The business is somewhat flexible, and it gives me my own income. Roy is a good man, and he makes enough to keep us comfortable. I work for the extras and so he and I can travel when we retire."

Quinton nodded and glanced at Wyatt. He wanted that kind of life. One where he was comfortable and had someone to rely on. Not someone who would take care of him, but instead someone who'd be there to work together with.

Callum began to fidget, and Quinton ate faster so he could finish before Callum decided he wanted his dinner.

Five minutes later he made up a bottle and fed Callum at the table while the others finished up. "You really seem to know what he wants," Lily observed. "He doesn't seem fussy to me."

"It seems the only one he's fussy for is his mother," Wyatt said, silently offering to take Callum. Quinton passed him over, and Wyatt fed him easily. Lily watched her son a little wistfully. "I'm going to go in the other room where it's quiet." He sat in the living room, and Quinton found himself alone with Lily once again.

"Do you love him?" Lily asked.

"Of course I do. He's my son."

Lily grinned. "No, I meant Wyatt," she said softly. "I've seen the way you look at him, and I know him. He's taken with you. Hell, he's in there feeding your son as though he were the most precious thing in the world. Or at least the second most precious." She sipped her water and held Quinton's gaze.

He wanted to squirm but forced himself not to. "What do you want me to say? And before you answer that, maybe this is something I should be talking about with Wyatt instead of with you." It was weird having Wyatt's mother asking if he was in love with Wyatt. Not that Quinton had a lot of experience with that particular emotion. The few times he had thought he was in love had turned out to be just lust or his own imagination making more of things than there was. His mother's version of love was anything that left her alone to live her own life, and that wasn't at all what he and Wyatt had.

"I think that's a really good idea," she said softly, but she had one of those looks in her eyes like she already knew and thought he was sort of dumb for not figuring it out. Not that she said anything of the sort. "You know it's okay to talk about your feelings."

Quinton shrugged. "Maybe I would if I had any idea what they were." He peered through the doorway into the other room, where Wyatt sat quietly feeling Callum. "Love hasn't been part of my life."

"Maybe it should be."

Quinton rolled his eyes. "Yeah, well, it isn't like I can go to the grocery store and pick up a package of it, or put it in a pot like a plant, water it, and have it grow."

She moved her chair around the table to sit right next to him. "Yes, you can. Lots of people think love is something that hits you and knocks you off your feet. That's just chemistry, and believe me, it fades like cheap perfume. Love is built on more than that. It's liking the other person and wanting them around. It's about missing them when they're gone. It's about wanting to do things for them just because it will make them happy and them doing little things that make you happy." She paused and took his hand. Quinton didn't pull it away because she seemed so earnest. "I fell in love with Wyatt's dad not because he was handsome, which I think he is, or because there was this wild chemistry, though there was some of that. Instead, it was the way he listened to me and made me feel special." She released his hand and stood up from the table. "I should get going."

"Okay…," Quinton said.

"You two kids don't need me, and I have to get home." He could see the urgency in her eyes. It was like she was suddenly missing her husband. "I'm glad I got to meet you." She patted his shoulder and said goodbye to Wyatt on her way through the house. Then the front door closed behind her, leaving Quinton to wonder what was truly going on between him and Wyatt.

AFTER EATING his dinner, Callum decided it was time to play, and he seemed determined not to go to sleep. Finally Quinton got him bathed and changed into his pajamas. Wyatt had turned down the lights, and the house was quiet. Quinton put Callum in his crib, set the baby monitor, and took it to the living room.

"Is he asleep?" Wyatt asked.

Quinton shook his head. "I hope he will be soon. He really wanted to fight it tonight." He sat next to Wyatt on the sofa and turned on the television. A few coos came through the monitor, and then it was quiet. He wanted to check, but he knew if Callum wasn't asleep, then he'd end up starting the bedtime routine all over again, and he was wiped out. The monitor remained silent, and Quinton shifted closer to Wyatt. "Your mother asked me a lot of stuff while you were in the living room."

Wyatt sighed. "She did?" Quinton nodded. "I knew I should have just stayed in there. Was it too bad?"

"Not really. Your mother loves you, and she wants the best for you. But she seems to have a lot of questions about how we feel for each other. I think she's afraid that you'll fall in love with me or something. Or worse, that I'll fall in love with you."

Wyatt stiffened. "She actually said that?"

"No." He lifted his head. "But I think she was trying to figure out how I felt about you and all. It was sort of uncomfortable, because you and I haven't even talked about that kind of stuff, and then she was asking if I loved you. I told her I didn't know because I haven't had a lot of experience with love, and then she told me about her and your dad before leaving. I think she just wanted to get away." Wyatt snickered and then laughed, making Quinton's head bounce slightly. "Is that funny?"

"No. Mom wanted to get home because she was talking about Dad, and those two still have the hots for each other." His flat belly bounced even more. "I always call now before I go home, because a couple months ago, I went home and walked in on Mom and Dad…. Let's just say there were sounds I never want to hear again, at least not from my parents. It's good that they still have a physical side to their relationship, but hearing it…." He shivered.

Quinton rolled his eyes. "That's nothing. At least it was your parents. Imagine being sixteen and hearing your mother and her current boyfriend. All I can say is it was a headboard-banging good time. Again… and again." He snickered and then laughed. "At least I knew my mother was happy, at least from the way she was praising God over and over. I never really thought of her as a religious person until then."

"Parents can scar their kids for life," Wyatt teased and tugged him closer. "But maybe sometimes I think our parents may have had the right idea." Before Quinton could ask him what he meant, Wyatt tugged him closer and kissed him. Quinton's mind instantly short-circuited, and he forgot about upcoming hearings and meeting Jennifer and the social worker tomorrow, simply concentrating on Wyatt. Maybe that was the magic here. The fact that Wyatt could make him forget, at least for a little while. And he could do it with such ease. It was frightening and exciting at the same time.

The cushions shifted under him as he pressed closer. The old couch had seen a lot over its lifetime, Quinton was pretty sure of that, but damn, it seemed that he and Wyatt were putting it through a real workout. "I wish I had more room." He paused, holding Wyatt's intensely heated gaze.

"I know. But we can't wake Callum, and somehow I don't think it's right to make love in the same room as the baby." Wyatt lay back on the cushions, pulling Quinton down on top of him. "But I want you."

Quinton nodded and then paused. "Did you mean what you just said?" Was it that easy? Could he just say what he felt?

"What?" Wyatt asked as though he hadn't even thought about the words.

"You just said… the way you said it," he said, not daring to break the connection between them. "That we're making love," he whispered as if everything would fall apart if he said it louder.

"Of course I meant it." Wyatt pulled him down into another kiss, and Quinton forgot about words and what Wyatt meant. Instead, he held on as Wyatt went ahead and proved what he was feeling with his hands, lips… hell, his entire body. He played Quinton as though he knew each and every reaction before Quinton could have it. They didn't dare make noise, but sound seemed like an unnecessary distraction. Communication came in many forms, and for the next hour or so, Wyatt and Quinton became masters of ecstatic nonverbal communication that left them breathless and completely worn out. Eventually they left their clothes strewn on the floor and silently headed to bed to spend the night in each other's arms.

# CHAPTER 13

"How DID it go with the social worker and Jennifer?" Wyatt asked as soon as Quinton called. So far the day had held nothing but frustration. They were getting nowhere with locating Remmy, and Wyatt was getting pressure to make headway in the case or the captain was going to have to bring in someone else. He could feel his chance at something more than traffic duty flying out the window.

Quinton sighed. "She was exactly the way we thought she would be: smug and ready to stick it to me. While her mother played with Callum, she and I talked, but all she kept saying was how she was going to bury my drug-using ass in court and that once everything was explained about the supposed car-theft incident, she was going to get Callum back and I was never going to see him again." Quinton seemed stronger than Wyatt would have thought he'd be. "It was just the sort of thing I had expected of her. Jennifer wasn't going to miss a chance to be mean."

"First thing, the charges against her aren't going away, and this hearing is for temporary placement. The judge doesn't get to dismiss those charges or change the fact that she's out on bail and that the reckless endangerment charges are still pending. Those are heard in regular court, not family court." Wyatt wanted to try to reassure Quinton. He could feel his pain almost as if it were his own. The thing was, he had come to love

Callum, and not seeing him again would leave a hole inside Wyatt too. "What did the lawyer say?"

"Pretty much the same thing you did, but that it was going to be an uphill battle anyway. Linda will be there with me at the hearing and seems really nice." It had taken a while for Quinton to get an appointment, but at least he had some legal help. "Anyway, Jennifer was no help at the visit. I tried goading her into talking, but she didn't take the bait."

"I see. Well, it was worth a try. Sorry you had to go through that for nothing." He hated putting Quinton in that position.

"Well, it wasn't exactly nothing." The wickedness in Quinton's voice gave him hope. "*She* didn't do any talking, but her phone did. Jennifer is in touch with Remmy. I saw a couple text messages come in from him while she was with Callum and the social worker. She must have gotten it back and left her phone on the table. Get a warrant for her phone and you'll get his phone number… and maybe some more information on him."

"She's also violated the terms of her bail," Wyatt said, already thinking about how he could use that against her. Placing the phone under his chin, he opened the form for a search warrant and began filling it in. "Were you able to read any of the messages, or did you just see that they came in?"

"I was able to read a few. Mostly they were about how he wanted to see her tonight. Stuff like that."

"Thanks," Wyatt said and added the details of what Quinton told him to the warrant request. Then he sent it to the chief for his approval. "Are you home with Callum?"

"Yeah. I have the doors locked tight, and we'll be waiting for you to come over." He seemed jittery, and Wyatt wanted to hurry to him, but he had to find a judge available to sign his warrant, and time was of the essence.

"Okay. I'll call you when I'm on my way. If you want to go to my place, then go. There's plenty of room there, and I don't think anyone will look for you there if that's what has you worried. My neighbor has a key, and I'll call him to let you in, and I'll see you there when I get home."

Quinton hung up, and Wyatt quickly called his neighbor and then set down his phone before going to find the chief.

Fortunately, he was still in his office, and Wyatt was able to fill him in and get his approval before sending the warrant on to the judge. He called as well and was notified that it had been approved. His inbox chimed, and he printed out the signed copy before calling Mark.

"I think we've got something," he told him. "I'll pick you up on the way." He was already out of the building and in the car, heading to Mark's, before the call ended.

JENNIFER ANSWERED the door at her aunt's home with her phone in her hand, which was convenient. "We have a warrant for all your electronic handheld devices," Mark told her and gently plucked the phone from her fingers.

"May I help you?" her aunt asked.

Mark explained what they were there for. "Are there any others of hers? We can take all the devices in the house if we need to," Mark said.

Her aunt paled. "I have a phone, and her uncle has one as well. There's an iPad that Jennifer uses." She got the iPad, and Mark took that too. He wrote up what they were taking and handed a receipt to Jennifer.

"Is that all?" Jennifer asked.

"What is the code to unlock them?" Wyatt asked, already working on the iPhone. This was damned frustrating.

"I don't have to tell you," Jennifer said smugly, crossing her arms over her chest.

"Then take her in for violating her bail. She can spend the night in jail, and a judge can determine whether she sits there until her trial. We know she's been in contact with someone possibly involved in a criminal enterprise. That's a violation of the terms of her bail." He was getting more and more pissed off at this woman.

Jennifer's aunt glared at her. "Two-one-two-two."

"Auntie!" Jennifer snapped.

"We are not getting involved in this mess. Your parents put up the bail and asked us to watch out for you. If you've done anything to put that money in jeopardy…." The fire in her eyes burned bright, and Jennifer probably knew her goose was cooked on that score.

Wyatt unlocked the phone and went right to the messages. He went through them on his way back to the car. He left Mark to deal with Jennifer and her aunt as he thumbed through the long message chain. They didn't talk about anything criminal, but it seemed they were to meet up in less than an hour at the Carlisle Diner.

"You hungry?" Wyatt asked Mark as soon as he climbed into the car. "She and Remmy were supposed to meet in less than an hour." He got on the phone to the captain, and they made a quick stop to change clothes and cars. Then they drove to the west side of town.

The Carlisle Diner was typical of the fifties or sixties, when it was originally built, complete with stainless steel on the outside and more stainless shining behind the seating counter. Booths lined the front of the room, which opened up to an addition that had been put on probably in the eighties. It was a pretty cool place, with huge windows and plenty of nostalgia. They got a booth with a clear view of the door as well as the front parking lot.

"What can I get you awhile?" the server asked in her classic central Pennsylvania vernacular. They each got a cup of coffee. Wyatt ordered a BLT and continued watching the front door and the time. He checked Jennifer's phone to see if there were any new messages, but it was quiet.

Finally, one came through saying that Remmy was on his way. Wyatt answered in a way he hoped Jennifer would and tensed. "He's on his way."

Mark lifted his attention from his phone. "I have other units out of sight. As soon as he comes in, I'll give the signal. We want to take him quietly and as easily as possible. Remember, we don't know if he's armed, and there are others in the restaurant."

Wyatt nodded. "Of course. My plan is to wait until he passes the table and simply arrest him. He can't know we're here."

"I put the fear of God into both Jennifer and her aunt that any communication with someone like Remmy Remington would not only result in a loss of Jennifer's possible freedom, but the court would then likely confiscate the bail money because of her behavior. I swear Jennifer's aunt looked about ready to shit herself."

"Good. Jennifer has caused enough trouble," Wyatt deadpanned.

Their server returned with drinks and then left again just as the front door opened. Remmy walked inside and looked both ways, most likely for Jennifer. The server returned and placed Wyatt's plate in front of him, and he thanked her just as Remmy passed behind her and walked toward the back of the restaurant.

"Is there anything else I can get you?" she asked.

Wyatt wanted to snap, but he kept his calm and said no. Fortunately, she went the opposite way, but Wyatt couldn't see Remmy. He was about to get up and try to find him when he reappeared again, striding forward toward the door.

"Remmy," Wyatt said as though they were long-lost friends. "It's been quite a while."

"Yeah, it has," he said absently, pausing just long enough to seem confused. "I'm looking for someone and I—"

Wyatt took one hand and whipped Remmy around, then cuffed him before he had a chance to resist. "We have a warrant, and you're under arrest for drug trafficking and distribution."

Mark was already on his feet in front in case Remmy decided to try to run. Not that he would get very far, but it was a precaution. "You're coming with us." He read him his rights and then led him out of the restaurant, and Wyatt put enough money on the table to cover the bill, disappointed that he hadn't gotten the opportunity to eat his sandwich.

"YOU GOT him," Captain Rogers said once they had booked their suspect and had him transferred to the county jail.

"Yes. We figured to let him sit overnight, and then we'll talk to him in the morning. Let him stew over what he wants to do and the kind of trouble he's in. Mark arranged to have his car towed to the county impound lot, and we'll go over it first thing, but it was the same car we chased." Wyatt sighed. It seemed they had finally caught a break in the case.

"You know this isn't over yet," the captain said. "We want the person in charge, and that's going to be even harder now that Remmy's in jail. If they communicated the way the others did, then it's possible he doesn't know we're making inroads."

"I don't think that's possible. This is the guy who handled the money. No one is going to do that blindly," Wyatt said. "He has to know who his boss is, and we're going to get him to talk."

He also wanted answers on how the pot came to be at Quinton's. It was Wednesday night, and the hearing was Friday. They were taking a chance talking to him tomorrow. Wyatt was tempted to try to speak to him tonight, but that would smell of desperation and maybe give Remmy the impression that he had some leverage. No, as much as Wyatt wanted answers, he was going to have to do this in a way that got them as much information as possible. He had a duty to the case just as much as he did to Quinton. His hope was that he could fulfill them both and wouldn't have to choose.


AFTER FINISHING up with the captain and the paperwork, Wyatt and Mark headed out. "I'll be here early so we can talk to him first thing. I doubt he'll get much sleep." Mark smiled and waved.

Wyatt got into his car and drove home. When he pulled up in front of the house, the front curtains fell back into place, and Quinton met him with Callum in his arms as soon as he walked in the door.

"We got him," Wyatt said.

"Did he confess to breaking in?" Quinton asked and then stepped back. "Or haven't you talked to him yet?" His excitement seemed to drain away. "Sorry. I've been on edge all day."

"It's okay. I'll be talking to him in the morning. He's got a lot to answer for." But there was also the possibility that he'd lawyer up and say nothing. Still, they had the car to go over, as well as all his electronic devices.

"But he doesn't have to say anything," Quinton said, and Wyatt nodded. "I know, the fifth amendment, right?"

"Yes." Wyatt put his weapon away and went into the kitchen. "Did you have anything to eat?"

"Callum has been ravenous, but I was waiting for you. I wasn't sure what you wanted me to do, and I didn't want to go rooting through your refrigerator."

"You should have gotten anything you wanted." Wyatt pulled open the refrigerator and realized it wouldn't have done much good. He hadn't been to the store lately, and there wasn't much, other than some leftovers from what his mother had brought. Wyatt thought about heating those up, but he ordered pizza for delivery instead and joined Quinton on the sofa. "Do you want a beer or something?"

"Sure," Quinton said, and Wyatt wished he'd thought of it before he left the kitchen. He got up and got a pair of bottles, opened them, and handed one to

Quinton before sitting down again. It felt damned good to be off his feet for a while.

"How was work?" Wyatt wanted to talk about anything other than this damned case. Yes, they were making progress, but he had hoped things would come together faster.

"Okay. We're working on the exterior of a lot of the buildings. I'm working with one of the masons this week to tuck-point some of the stone. That's a messy job, but it needs to be done to make sure the buildings stay secure. The older ones are well over a hundred years old, so they need to be looked after on a regular basis. I've been told that they're happy with my work, so I'll be with them for the next few months, and in the winter I'll return to plumbing. The plan is to get me trained so I can eventually be registered, and then I'll get a good raise. It takes a few years, but once I can join the union, I'll be a lot better off." He bounced Callum lightly on his knees, getting smiles.

"He's pretty amazing." Wyatt tickled his belly, and Callum grinned a gummy smile. "Yes, you are." He was trying to spend a few seconds in the here and now, knowing that Quinton was stretched so thin that if anything else happened, he was likely to shatter into pieces.

THE PIZZA arrived, and Callum was still going strong. Wyatt held him so Quinton could eat. They were both getting pretty good at eating with one hand and holding the baby with the other. After eating, Quinton got Callum changed into his jammies. After another bottle, Quinton put Callum to bed in the porta-crib Wyatt had set up in the guest room for foster babies.

"I know you're nervous," Wyatt told him.

"Of course I am," Quinton snapped, and then apologized and sat next to him. "I'm scared to death. The social worker is going to be coming to my house tomorrow to do another check before the hearing. I know it's fine, but I don't know how much more of this I can take. Every day I worry just a little bit more. We can't prove who put those drugs in my house, so Jennifer is going to use that against me, just like we thought she was. The judge is going to have to take it seriously because it's their job to, and Callum is going to go back to the care of a mother who left him unattended in the car so he could be kidnapped." His hands shook.

Wyatt pulled him into a hug. There was nothing else he could do, and it was the most helpless feeling in the world. To make matters worse, he knew on some level that he was the one who had let Quinton down. If Wyatt had been better at his job, he'd have found the evidence they needed. "I'm sorry." Those were the only words he had.

Quinton shrugged. "It's not your fault."

Wyatt appreciated that Quinton wanted him to feel better too, but he knew that wasn't true. This was his fault, and he needed to fix it. There had to be a way to prove what they needed to. The most likely route was through Remington, and they had him in custody. If Wyatt handled it right, he might be able to get him to talk or even accidentally admit that he had been in the house to help Jennifer. Logic dictated that was likely, but with what they had now, it would be a stretch to use it in the hearing. "Do you want to watch something on television?"

"We can, sure," Quinton answered absently. Wyatt turned it on and sat next to him, an arm around

Quinton's shoulders. Wyatt had no intention of letting him go, and he needed to try to make things better. "I know I'm being a downer."

"You're worried. That's only natural." Wyatt used the remote and turned off the television. It was only providing background noise, since it was pretty obvious that neither of them was going to actually watch what was on. "And I'm going to do everything I can to help you."

"I know." Quinton turned to him. "But there's only so much you can do. You can't beat the guy with a rubber hose to make him talk." He grinned. "Can you?" Wyatt knew he was joking. "I know, use the rack or the iron maiden." Wyatt rolled his eyes. "Thumb screws, the boot? Chinese water torture?" With each one he mentioned, Quinton smiled, his humor not really covering his worry very well.

"No. I can't use any of them, and it's impressive the number of medieval torture devices you're able to name."

"It's a gift," Quinton deadpanned. "I know you have to follow the rules, and I wouldn't want you to do anything else. But a guy can dream, can't he?"

Wyatt snorted. "I don't tend to dream about torturing suspects." Maybe it was time to try another tack. He leaned close to Quinton's ear. "I tend to dream about a certain father and the kinds of things I'd like to do to him that are adults-only."

A shiver went through Quinton.

"And damn, his big blue eyes get huge when he's just about to come, and every time it seems like a surprise."

"Wyatt…," Quinton whispered. "What are you doing?"

"What do you think?" Wyatt whispered back. "I'm trying to seduce you." He sat back, smoldering at Quinton. "I figured that maybe I could take your mind off things for a little while. And I think you'd like it."

"Do you think this is the time for stuff like that?" Quinton asked.

Wyatt chuckled. "We're guys. It's always time for stuff like that." He waggled his eyebrows, and Quinton smiled and then pounced. Wyatt was still laughing until the moment before Quinton's lips touched his. From then on there was nothing to laugh about. Wyatt pulled him close and cradled him as things grew more intense by the second. "Bedroom?"

Quinton hummed some sort of answer, but his lips pressed down again, taking Wyatt's breath away. Maybe it was the worry, but Quinton seemed even more intense than usual, which was never a bad thing. Wyatt slowly sat up, wrapping Quinton's legs around his waist, and then he stood, cupping Quinton's jeans-clad butt as he carried him to the bedroom.

To say that Wyatt was excited was the understatement of the century, and from the intensity washing off Quinton, he had turned from worried to live wire. Wyatt had no illusions that this was going to change anything in the long run. All he wanted was to make Quinton happy and take his mind off the worry for a while, and maybe then Quinton could sleep. Wyatt set him on the side of the bed and pulled Quinton's T-shirt over his head. He got his own off as well before pressing Quinton back onto the bed.

"Wyatt…," Quinton whispered.

Wyatt yanked open his jeans, tugged them off, and dropped them to the floor. "I want you… now," he growled. He pulled off Quinton's briefs and sucked his long, thick cock between his lips.

Quinton quivered and whimpered as Wyatt took more of him, bobbing his head. "Jesus...." Quinton groaned, and damned if that wasn't the sexiest sound ever. "Don't stop," he whispered.

Wyatt didn't intend to. He ran his tongue around the base of the head before taking all of Quinton that he could. Damn, he was sexy as hell. His musky taste, the whimpers, even the way his smooth skin slipped under his hands was amazing. Quinton lay still, his eyes wide, mouth hanging open, and he shook slightly with excitement. Now that was perfection, knowing Wyatt could make Quinton lose himself this way.

"What are you doing?" Quinton whimpered when Wyatt pulled back. Wyatt took a few seconds to shuck the rest of his clothes and climb on the bed. "Oh...."

"Yeah." He kissed Quinton hard, the energy in the room zipping even higher. "What do you like?" He realized that the two of them had never talked about positions in bed, and Wyatt desperately needed to know. "What is it that you think of when you close your eyes?" Color rose in Quinton's cheeks. "What is it?"

"Well, I imagine looking down at you while I slide deep inside you," Quinton said.

Wyatt grinned. "Baby, that's okay. I tend to be versatile. So...." He tugged Quinton closer, drawing him up, and Wyatt lay back on the bed.

"You mean it?" Quinton said. Wyatt reached into the nightstand and handed Quinton a condom and a packet of lube. His hand shook as he took them.

"But I don't want to hurt you," Quinton said.

Wyatt drew closer. "You won't. Just use plenty of slick and you'll be fine."

God, they really should have talked about this earlier, but Quinton knew what to do, judging by the way he used his fingers with enough skill to make Wyatt's eyes cross and have him panting for breath… and that was just the preliminary. Quinton left him breathless—the stretch, the intensity of being taken deep, the zing as Quinton's cock slid past his prostate, sending ripples through him that never seemed to end. Then there were Quinton's eyes, wide in wonder as he leaned over him.

Wyatt wound his arms around Quinton's neck and tugged him down and into a kiss as Quinton slid deep and held there. "Wow," Wyatt breathed. Thankfully Quinton took it slow to begin with, letting Wyatt get used to him. Then they moved together, just fast enough to rev the engines a little, but not too fast to race to the finish line. The slow build was amazing, and Wyatt held Quinton tightly, their gazes boring into each other.

Quinton could see into his soul, Wyatt knew it, just like he got a glimpse into Quinton's. And what he saw was light and care, the perfect lover and parent. Someone Wyatt would be lucky to have in his life. He kissed Quinton hard, trying to convey all his feelings into action. Wyatt's words fell short, and he needed some way to tell Quinton just how he felt about him. "Don't stop… don't ever stop." For a second he wondered if he was talking about the sex or about the warmth that surrounded him, and Wyatt realized it was both.

"I don't intend to," Quinton whispered, kissing him again before straightening up, giving Wyatt a full view of his lean frame. Damn, that was an impressive sight, and it only increased his passion. Wyatt sure as hell hoped nothing happened and the house didn't fall down around them, because he swore he'd barely notice. Quinton was taking him for a ride that he hoped he never saw the end of.

Wyatt held his legs up, knees bent, with Quinton between, stretched and lean, hips flexing, the bed rocking slightly. The room filled with the sounds of passion, skin on skin, deep breathing, the scent of sweat and male love filling the air, driving the ecstasy higher with each inhalation. His skin grew sensitive wherever Quinton touched him, electric sparks raced up his spine, and yet somehow Wyatt was able to control himself. He didn't want to do his imitation of a teenager, but Quinton hammered at his control, and soon enough it hung by a thread. His head spun and he tried to focus his eyes, but all he could do was place his pleasure in Quinton's hands and give himself over to it. Once he did, a whole new level of pleasure opened up and he just flew.

The tingling became more powerful and the pressure intense. Like a rubber band, Wyatt's control snapped and his release barreled into him, taking him on a ride as high as the clouds—one he hoped he'd stay on forever.

Wyatt held Quinton close when he collapsed forward. They were warm and covered with sweat, but he didn't mind. Athletic sex had that effect, and damn, but Wyatt loved some good loving. He believed in being gentle, but there was no reason that passion should be contained.

"Damn," Wyatt breathed.

"Was that good?" Quinton asked sheepishly.

Wyatt held him tighter. "It was way better than good." He rubbed Quinton's back, shivering slightly when their bodies disconnected. Quinton shifted away, the air cool on his skin while the condom was disposed of. Then Quinton tugged him up out of the bed.

"I think we could both use a shower before bed."

"You do, huh?" Wyatt slipped his arms around Quinton's waist, his chest to Quinton's back. "You know what showers mean? Slippery, wet…."

"I see." Quinton slowly turned around. "What are you, a machine? Are you ready to go again already? It's only been, like, five minutes."

"See what you do to me." He lowered his gaze to where his cock was already growing hard again.

Quinton chuckled. "Okay, then. How about you get things ready in the bathroom and I'll peek in on Callum and then join you."

Wyatt agreed and hurried to get the water running and the towels out. He figured his job was to try to keep Quinton from dwelling on what was going to come next. But that was only part of it. He also needed to come through and nail whoever had tried to frame Quinton. Distraction was one thing, but a true positive resolution was a whole other issue.

# CHAPTER 14

QUINTON'S PHONE had been silent all morning, and Quinton thought he was going to go out of his mind. The hardest part was that he needed to stay focused on what he was doing or the pipes he was supposed to be joining to complete the emergency repair would leak all over the damned place and then he'd get in trouble for another reason. Somehow he forced himself to focus on the task in front of him and not on the fact that Wyatt hadn't called him.

There were many possible reasons Wyatt hadn't called. Maybe he was chasing some leads and couldn't. Still, he had hoped that Wyatt would let him know if their suspect had talked. No news was good news, he kept telling himself, and went back to work.

At lunch, he nearly jumped a mile when his phone vibrated in his pocket. He shifted his weight as he sat in the red Adirondack chair under a sprawling oak so he could get at the phone. It was his mother, and he rolled his eyes before answering.

"Hey, Mom," he said gently.

"You never call," she mumbled softly, and he wondered if she was hungover.

"Well, I've been busy. I'm working now, and after work I pick up Callum from day care. Then he keeps me busy until it's time for him to go to bed." He was getting a little worn down, but he wasn't going to tell her that. "What can I do for you?" He took a bite of his bologna sandwich and closed his eyes. Quinton loved it out in the quad where it was quiet. With only summer classes, the campus was largely empty, and that meant he could sit under the trees.

"You still have the kid?" she asked. Quinton scrunched his eyebrows. "You know you have a choice. You could just let his mother take care of him and you could go back to your own life without a kid weighing you down. You're young. You can have more kids once you settle down properly." By which she meant with a woman. He could hear her inhale and knew that sound. She was obviously smoking again, all her vices coming forward.

"Yeah, Mom, I'm well aware of that. Except I *want* to raise Callum. I know that seems like a foreign concept to you, but he deserves that."

She snorted. "Yeah, like any kid deserves to be raised by a gay man." The derision rolled off her. "You can be whatever you want to be, but that don't mean you need to be raising babies."

"What did you call for?" he asked. It was either get off this subject or they were going to have a shouting match over the phone, and he didn't want that while he was at work. Also, he came out here to relax, not that she cared.

"I'm a little short this month, and I was hoping you could help me out with a hundred or so." She said it as though she actually expected Quinton to hand it over like it was her due.

"Sorry. All the money I have is going to take care of Callum. There's nothing extra." Not that he had any intention of giving anything to her. "Maybe if you didn't drink so much and smoke like a chimney, you'd have some money. Hell, I bet the hundred you want is so you can get a carton of cigarettes and a fifth." He knew her so damned well. "You're going to have to look somewhere else."

"You little shit. I brought you into this world and raised you." Now he knew she'd been drinking.

"Like that's going to get you what you want." He knew he should have just let the call go to voicemail and then deleted it. Nothing good ever came out of these conversations. "I need to go back to work. Sorry I can't help you. What about the guy you're seeing? Who's next through your revolving door?"

"Don't be so high and mighty. I know you got a court date tomorrow. Maybe I'll go in and tell them about the kind of kid you were. That will scare a judge."

Quinton felt cold for a second. He should have expected something like this from her. Everything was always about what she could get out of it. "Then I'll explain to the judge the kind of mother I have. And you'll have just proved it." He always had to be one step ahead of her. It was sad that a win with his mother was keeping her away. God, he really hadn't had much of a chance. It was a miracle he hadn't ended up in prison or worse with her as a role model. His mother only made him want to be the best parent he could be in order to break the cycle and give Callum the chance at a better life. "Bye, Mom." He ended the call and put his phone back in his pocket, figuring she would move on to some other poor sucker to try to get the money. God, he thought, a call from your mother shouldn't seem like the wave of death in choppy water.

Quinton finished eating and then threw away the garbage as he headed back to work. He checked his phone to find a text from Wyatt. *Still working on it* was all it said. He responded with *thanks* and returned to work. At least he'd heard something, and he had faith in Wyatt. Even if he was scared half to death.

By the time he was done with work, he hadn't heard anything more. Quinton picked up Callum at day care and was greeted by his happy boy, who grinned when he saw him. There was nothing better than that happy face.

"He was such an angel all day," his attendant said, and Quinton grinned at his son. He thanked her and carried Callum out to his old car, then made sure he was secured in the back seat before going home, where he changed Callum and fed him, soothing himself by pacing with him as Callum slept in his arms.

The front door opened, and Quinton met Wyatt in the hall. He smiled and then put Callum into his crib, calming his nerves before returning to the living room, where Wyatt sat on the edge of the sofa. "What happened?"

"He's refusing to say anything," Wyatt said. "He won't answer any questions of any kind. All he does is sit in the interview room with his arms crossed over his chest. He asked for a lawyer, and that was the most he spoke all day."

Quinton felt like a gaping maw had opened up in front of him. "What am I going to do?" He swallowed hard.

"Kip is going to come in and be available to explain what he believes and what he's working on. He doesn't believe that the pot was yours, if for no other reason than that has to be the stupidest hiding place on earth. It's obvious that it was planted there, and with the tip-off phone call…."

"Yeah. But the judge isn't going to be able to write it off. And that may be enough for them to give Callum back to Jennifer, especially if her parents step in to back her up. If I lose Callum at any point, then the chances of me getting custody pretty much go through the floor. I know that."

Wyatt shook his head. "I wish I could do more for you. And I'm going to keep trying, but I don't know if I can get this tough nut to crack in time." He bit his lower lip. "Mark tried to get through to him for most of the afternoon, but there is only so much you can do when a suspect refuses to say anything at all. And damn, I really wanted him to say something we could use. I watched the guy through the glass all day, and he did nothing but sit there. The few times he spoke, it was to say that he had nothing to say."

"Then I guess all I can do is my best and hope it's good enough."

"Jennifer is still only out of jail by the skin of her teeth, and that will work in your favor. She's one tiny mistake from having her bail revoked, and the judge at the hearing will know that."

Quinton nodded. "Yeah. But I need to put the nail in her coffin as quickly as possible. It's my best chance to be able to raise Callum, and if he's to have any chance at all, then that's what's got to happen." He leaned against Wyatt and buried his face in his chest.

Wyatt cradled him in his arms, holding tightly. Quinton tried not to shake. He had to try to keep his wits about him, but it was hard as the clouds overhead grew darker.

# CHAPTER 15

WYATT SPENT the entire night holding Quinton and worrying. Quinton finally got to sleep well after midnight. Wyatt changed and fed Callum when he fussed an hour later, then got him back to bed so Quinton could sleep.

Not that Wyatt could sleep much either. The case and the details kept running through his head. There had to be something he was missing, and what kept bothering him was that it was probably right under his nose and he just wasn't seeing it. Finally he nodded off and woke with the first of the sun. Wyatt slipped out of bed and gently stroked Quinton's hair.

"What time is it?" Quinton muttered.

"Very early. Get some rest. Callum is still asleep, and I'm going to go in to work and try again." He kissed him, dressed, and went right into the station. At the desk he was using, he went over all the details he knew.

"We have to find something."

"Did you sleep here?" Mark asked as he set down his things. "You were still here when I left yesterday."

"No. I got here an hour ago. Quinton's hearing is today at one, and I'm trying to find something to help. I know that someone was in his home and planted the pot. I know it, but I can't prove it. That's what I'll need to wrap this in a bow." He sat back in the chair. "We found Remington's prints on the bag, but that doesn't mean he put it there, only that he handled the bag at some point and that he seems to be the last one to. Quinton's prints were absent."

"Yeah. But that just tells us he didn't handle the bag. Kip's report says that it hadn't been there long, and we know that Quinton was out on a walk because you saw him coming back. Hell, even I'm convinced that he didn't do it. But for the court, we need proof." Mark paused. "All we need is evidence that someone who should never have been in that house was actually there."

Wyatt was stunned. "Oh my God." He stood quickly, rolling his chair back. "Callum was in bed this morning, and I leaned over the crib to look at him before I left." His heart raced a little faster. "We need to go... now."

"What?" Mark asked.

Wyatt was already on his way out, telling the desk sergeant where he was going.

"When you place a baby in a crib, you use both hands and gently place them inside. It's what I've seen Quinton do, and it's what I do. However, this morning when I took a look, I leaned over the crib and placed my hand on the rail. What if our intruder did the same thing?" He was already at the car. "I need to dust that rail for prints and see if we get anything."

"Wyatt, hold up. You said you leaned on the rail this morning. I bet Quinton has as well. Any prints are going to be covered up and smudged all to hell." Mark put his hand on his shoulder. "You need to think about this."

"I am. Didn't you notice yesterday? Those few times Remington did talk, when you slid the paper and pen over to him, he pretty much ignored them, except for one thing. He played with the pen—in his left hand.

So if he leaned over the crib, he would have placed something inside with his left hand and used the right to steady himself. I'm right-handed, so are you… and so is Quinton." He got in the car and waited until Mark had closed his door before hurrying over to Quinton's.

WYATT HAD hoped Quinton would still be home, but he wasn't there. He messaged him and then used the key Quinton had given him to let himself inside and went right to the bedroom. He pulled on gloves and removed the bedding from the crib. "You'd better do this. That way, you can be the one to testify if needed. It will carry more weight than if I do it."

Mark nodded and got down on his knees, pulling out the fingerprint kit. He dusted along the right side of the rail and got basically smudges before moving on.

Wyatt wanted to help, but he knew this had to be done carefully, so he leaned against the door and tried not to tap his foot impatiently. "Take a look," Mark said with a smile and handed Wyatt a flashlight. "Don't even breathe." He shone the light on the underside of the crib rail at two nearly perfect fingerprints right between the rails. Mark took photographs and then lifted the prints, transferred them to a card, and slid them into an evidence bag.

Only then did they both begin to breathe again. "We need to get these run… and now." Wyatt checked his watch. It was after noon, and the hearing was scheduled at the Family Law Center in less than an hour. "The lab will take too long, and going back to the station is going to eat up time."

Mark pulled out his phone. "Kip, it's Mark. I need a favor. Is Carter working today? We need a verified fingerprint match, and I'm here with Wyatt, but he's too close...." Mark paused, already heading for the door. "We're on our way." He hung up the phone. "Carter is there, and he'll be ready for us. Call the captain and tell him what's going on, and don't you dare touch anything. I want the chain of evidence on this as spotless as my mama's Sunday dishes. You drive, and put on the damned siren. Time is ticking."

THEY WERE admitted to the Carlisle Police Station and shown to Carter's bank of computers. He scanned the print from the card and signed the evidence register. Once that was done, it took mere minutes to verify the identity the print, and with the identity of the intruder in hand, Wyatt checked his watch one more time before thanking Carter.

Mark drove while Wyatt called Quinton, but he only got his voicemail. It was nearly two, and he was likely already in the hearing. Dammit. They had to get to the center of town. Fortunately, they were both familiar with the traffic patterns, and Mark got them there relatively quickly. After passing through security, they rode the elevator up the Family Law Center and went inside.

"May I help you?" the receptionist asked with a serious smile.

"Yes. We are here for the Jackson/Winters hearing," Wyatt explained.

"That began an hour ago, and only the parties directly involved are allowed." She narrowed her gaze. "What is this about?"

"We have evidence that the judge is going to want to hear. It's important." Mark flashed her his best smile.

"You know this is just a preliminary placement hearing," she said. "Okay. Let me call back. Just a minute." She seemed put out, but she made the call and directed them to the hearing room. It looked like a cross between a conference room and a court chamber. The judge sat behind a raised desk, with tables and a few chairs on either side in front.

"Gentlemen," the judge said as they entered. "We were just about to wrap up. I have heard from both the mother and the father." Wyatt turned to Quinton, who was as pale as a sheet, sitting next to his lawyer, head bowed. Wyatt hated that he looked that miserable. He wished he had been faster.

"Thank you, Your Honor," Mark said. "But I believe we can make this decision very easy for you." Wyatt stood to the side and let Mark do the talking. "If you'll permit us."

She seemed skeptical, and Wyatt expected Mark to be told to sit and wait his turn. "Very well."

"Your Honor, I swear that what I am about to tell you is the truth, the whole truth, and nothing but the truth." Mark smiled as the judge nodded.

"Thank you for that. I'll take that as your oath. Now, please continue." She motioned them to seats, and Wyatt sat while Mark continued forward and sat off to the side as a witness. In these hearings, the judge usually led the questioning.

"In the interest of full disclosure, my partner is involved with Quinton. They have a personal relationship, which is why I have been taking the lead in this part of our investigation. I'm sure you are aware of the illicit drug distribution center that was broken up recently. We are in charge of that investigation, and by coincidence that investigation and this custodial

hearing have overlapped. Yesterday we took into custody one of the leaders of that center, a Mr. Raymond
Remington...."

Mark continued speaking, but Wyatt heard Jennifer's sharp intake of air. Wyatt stared at her as Mark
went on.

"Then I take it that what you wish to present has
to do with the illicit substances found in Mr. Jackson's
home."

"Yes, Your Honor. The suspect we took into custody has refused to cooperate, but we have booked and
fingerprinted him, just like when Jennifer Winters was
taken into custody. When you place a baby in the crib,
you use both hands, but when the suspect placed the
drugs in it, they used only one, and the other rested on
the railing. To be specific, their right hand rested on the
railing." Mark paused and then turned to Jennifer. "You
tried to frame Quinton to get some of the heat off you."

Wyatt could finally breathe.

"You got the marijuana from Mr. Remington, a
man you've been seeing, and we can link your asso-
ciation through your phones." Now it was Jennifer's
turn to pale, and Wyatt loved every second of it. "We
can prove that by his fingerprints on the bag. I suspect
you wore a glove to put the bag in the crib, but you
forgot your other hand." Mark placed the evidence bag
and the printout that Carter had certified in front of the
judge.

"I see...."

"Those prints could be from any time I visited,"
Jennifer said.

Quinton quietly spoke to his attorney, who nodded.

"Your Honor, Jennifer has never set foot in my place since she had Callum. I always picked him up at her apartment or at her aunt's."

Wyatt was relieved that Quinton had more color and sat straighter. When Quinton turned, Wyatt nodded, as if to say, *I told you I would do my very best*. He only wished he had thought of it sooner.

"Furthermore, Your Honor, the state police will be referring her to the DA for charges of breaking and entering, as well as possession of a controlled substance, among others. Those charges result from activities while she was on bail."

There was no need for Mark to continue. The judge would know that bail would be revoked and that Jennifer would immediately return to jail and wasn't going to be granted bail again. Then it would be up to the court to determine how long she would be incarcerated. But it would be a while.

"Thank you, Trooper," the judge said and turned to Jennifer's side of the room.

Jennifer and her lawyer talked, with Jennifer becoming agitated.

"We have no questions," Jennifer's lawyer said with a shrug. God, Wyatt could tell that poor man wanted as far away from her as possible. There was nothing either of them could do. No judge was going to grant custody, even temporary, to a mother in jail.

"Then my decision is an easy one. Mr. Jackson has cared for his son for the past two weeks, and the social worker reports have been glowing. Apparently, Mr. Jackson, you take your role as father very seriously, and I'm glad to hear it. Temporary custody is granted to you, and a decision on permanent placement will be made in six months." She leaned forward. "In many cases before me, the choice is between the better of two parents. In this case, there was only one true parent present." She banged her gavel. "As for you, Miss Winters, I remand you to the custody of the state police pending charges and the revocation of bail." She turned to the door. "Please get a bailiff and have them place her under arrest." Then she stood and left the courtroom. A few minutes later a bailiff stepped into the room and cuffed a fuming Jennifer.

Fortunately, she didn't fight, but she turned to Quinton with a look of sheer death. "You can't get away with this. There is no way you're going to take my baby away from me. This should be you."

"Breaking and entering is a crime, as is trying to frame someone else," Wyatt told her. The door closed behind her. Once she had gone, Wyatt came forward to stand next to Quinton.

"You did it," Quinton said softly. "I don't know how."

"I told you I would do my best. I'm just sorry it took so long." They shared a smile, and then Quinton thanked his attorney.

"You're very welcome." She shook Quinton's hand and left the room through the back door.

"Are you ready to take Callum home?" Wyatt asked Quinton. "I'm still on duty and need to go back to work." Or else he'd have kissed Quinton within an inch of his life. "But I'll see you tonight, and we'll celebrate." He smiled. "I'll walk you and Callum out." He motioned toward the door.

Quinton paused and then turned back and took a step toward Jennifer's stunned mother. "Mrs. Winters," he said gently, "I want you to know that this has nothing to do with you. And I won't stop you from seeing Callum. I want him to know his grandparents."

Her lower lip quivered. She lifted her gaze from the floor, and Wyatt tensed, not sure of her reaction. "Thank you." She turned back toward the door before picking up her purse to go. "I think maybe the court made the right decision." Then she passed out of the room.

Quinton stayed locked in place, and Wyatt gently placed his hand on his back. "That was so lucky," he whispered. "I got lucky."

Wyatt didn't say anything, but he wanted to argue. Not many people would have done what Quinton had done. Most people just didn't have hearts that big and caring. Wyatt figured he was the lucky one, and he needed to figure out how he was going to show Quinton just how lucky he thought he was to have him and Callum in his life. And it had to be something as special as Quinton was.


"WHAT ARE we going to do about our suspect?" Mark asked once they were back at the station. Wyatt figured that in another day or two, he was going to be back on patrol either way, but he really wanted to get to the people who were truly behind the distribution.

"Charge him with everything we can think of. If he isn't going to give us the name of the people involved, then put him on the hook for all of it. We can contact the district attorney as well. The lawyer may try to make a deal, but we make sure that he has to tell us what he knows or we go for it all." Wyatt wasn't sure how much this would net them, but he had to try. "We should also get to Jennifer to find out how much she knows about her boyfriend. She's scared half to death about now and is looking at some pretty serious time, especially after being charged with breaking and entering with malicious intent." God, there were times when he loved the nuances of the law.

"I agree. Which one do you want to take?" Mark grinned as if he didn't already know.

"I think I'll contact Kip and work with him. I bet if Jennifer sees me it will flip her out. Who knows— anger often makes people say things they never would otherwise."

"Excellent. And we'll see what kind of boyfriend our suspect is," Mark agreed.

Wyatt made a call to Kip, who was more than happy to work with him. Mark went off to work on their suspect. Wyatt had gotten a good result on one half of the case, and now he needed to figure out how to wrap this thing up and tie a bow on it.

Wyatt hurried out to meet Kip at the county jail, which was about ten minutes away. He parked and presented himself at the desk.

Kip came out almost right away. "Glad you could get here so soon. She just got back from the courthouse about ten minutes ago." He swiped his card to let them into the back area. "How are things with Quinton?"

Wyatt paused and couldn't help smiling. "Good. We got the evidence, and he has temporary custody. The judge will make a permanent decision in six months."

"That's good, but I meant the two of you. But from that grin, I'd say you were pretty happy." Wyatt wasn't going to deny that for a second. "So, fill me in on what you're trying to do?"

"In a nutshell, she was the one who planted those drugs." Wyatt explained what they'd found. "We expected to find indication of her boyfriend, who is also in custody."

"And you want to play her off against him?" Kip asked. "Good, I can do that. I take it he isn't talking."

Wyatt shook his head. "Not a single word. But if we can make her angry because he isn't helping her…. It's likely she got the drugs from him, and maybe it was all his idea." Wyatt grinned.

"How do you want to play this?"

Wyatt grinned and explained his idea. Kip's eyes widened, and then his lips turned upward. "Damn, Wyatt, I never pictured you as someone that devious. She'll be brought in soon. Let's do this."

# CHAPTER 16

QUINTON WAS happy, even if Callum seemed sniffly. He lay on his old sofa with Callum on his chest, rising and falling with each breath he took, sound asleep for the first time since he'd picked him up at day care. After leaving court when Wyatt returned to work, Quinton had dropped off Callum and then had gone to work with a load off his chest. Callum was his for the next six months, and he hoped permanently.

A knock on the front door had him grinding his teeth, and he got up slowly, holding Callum to him so he didn't wake. Sleep was best for him, and Quinton was hoping the little guy would feel better. He opened the door to a Black woman with her hand raised to knock. "Can I help you?" he whispered.

She nodded and smiled. "Actually, I'm here to help you," she said.

Quinton groaned. "Ma'am, if you want to know if I've accepted Jesus Christ as my savior, then no. As a gay man, I've had enough religion to last me the rest of my life. I've already been asked to buy raffle tickets, and all I'm trying to do is keep the baby asleep." He stepped back to close the door.

"I'm from Child Services," she said, and Quinton sighed.

"I'm sorry. He came home from day care with the sniffles, and it's taken an hour to get him to sleep. Then when I do, someone knocks on the door. I've had folks determined to save my soul, and another group selling raffle tickets." He was so tired. "Please come in." He stepped back and let her close the door.

Callum shifted and began to fuss. Quinton rocked slightly to try to soothe him, and thankfully Callum settled back to sleep. "What can I help you with?"

"We understand that you received temporary custody of Callum today. The day care grant that we've been using only covers emergency situations." She sat in the chair across from him and pulled out some forms. "Donald wanted to be proactive and get the forms filled out for a more permanent day care grant. He also thought that you might qualify for some of our other programs." She talked him through the forms, and he signed them when she was done.

"Thank you."

"I also brought some supplies for you." She left and returned with a couple cases of diapers and packages of wipes, with Wyatt following her inside.

"Hey, Janine," he said brightly.

"Wyatt. How are you doing?" she asked, and they talked a minute while Callum began to fuss. Wyatt took him as easy as anything, rocking him in his arms, and damned if Callum didn't drop right back to sleep. Not that Quinton could blame him. There was no safer place that he knew of than sleeping in Wyatt's arms.

"Quinton and I have been seeing each other," Wyatt explained to Janine.

She patted Wyatt's arm. "You and Mark did good work today. Talk of that hearing has already made it through the office." She smiled, her eyes bright. "You sure as heck waited for the last minute, though."

"You don't know the half of it," Wyatt told her. "But things worked out for Quinton and for this little guy here." He looked down at Callum, and his policeman's expression melted away. His eyes grew softer, and the lines around his mouth smoothed out.

"Well, I'll leave you and get this paperwork filed right away. Don't worry about anything. I'll be in touch in a week or so to go over things." She left the house, and Quinton collapsed into one of the chairs.

"I don't know how much more I can take with social workers, courts, and God knows what else. I just want a quiet life with Callum." He lifted his gaze. "And you."

Wyatt sat down. "That's good, because I have a surprise for you."

Quinton blinked. "Your mother and father are coming to dinner?" He was kidding, but with the way he felt, that was about the worst thing that could happen. They had settled on tomorrow night to go to their house. All that Quinton could think about was that it was the weekend, and he didn't have to get up for work for the next two days.

"That's tomorrow." Wyatt placed Callum in his carrier and got him buckled in. "Get his diaper bag and pack something for the two of you tonight." He moved closer to Quinton. "Okay?"

Quinton nodded, unable to move under the spell of Wyatt's intense eyes. "I'll be right back." He went to the bedroom and packed the diaper bag with some clothes and extra supplies and got formula from the kitchen. Then he got an old duffel bag and put in clothes for himself. He wondered what kind of surprise Wyatt had in mind, but the best one he could get right now was a full night's sleep. Not like that was going to happen, but still, a guy could dream.

Once he was packed, he met Wyatt in the living room. "I already checked the doors, and my car is right out front." He smiled and leaned forward to kiss him. "Let's go."

"Are we going to a hotel or something? Because I'll need a lot more than this," Quinton asked, but Wyatt shook his head. "Okay, then."

Wyatt drove them to his house and carried Callum inside and right upstairs. Quinton followed and gasped when he found the spare bedroom all set up for Callum. The light blue walls were perfect, and Quinton put his hand over his mouth at the white crib and matching dresser with a duck-shaped lamp on it. "Where did this come from?"

"Mom and Dad picked it up for me, and Dad put it together. They found the lamp at a secondhand store and snapped it up." He smiled at Callum in his carrier. "I wanted to do something to tell you that I want both you and Callum in my life. That you make me happier than I ever thought was possible."

Quinton didn't quite know what to say.

"I made up this room so that Callum will have a proper place to sleep when you come over, and eventually maybe this could be his room... when you're ready."

Quinton swallowed. "Are you asking us to move in here?" His head spun a little. He had only known Wyatt for a matter of weeks, and what surprised him was that he was ready.

"If that's what you want to do. But I think I'm telling you that both you and Callum have a place here in my home." Wyatt stepped closer. "And in my heart. I want the two of you to be part of my life. I know that there are still many things coming up and that this fight with Jennifer isn't over." He drew Quinton into his arms, the warmth of his hug surrounding him like he was meant to be there.

"You feel right to me too," Quinton said, lifting his head to Wyatt's gaze. "I think I fell in love with you when you first smiled at me and Callum at that parenting class. There was something there that said that you saw us... me. You saw me, and not just as Callum's daddy, but me." He buried his head in Wyatt's neck, inhaling deeply. "So few people have ever seen me. My mother sees me as a potential money machine, even though I don't have any. My friends just see me as someone to go along with their craziness." He stopped.

"Well, I see you as a parent, a partner." Wyatt leaned close to his ear. "A lover." That word sent a zip racing down his spine. "A friend. I see you as sexy and hot. You're a lot of things, and I see all of them." He stood still, just holding him. "We all want to be seen and cared for."

"Yeah, and I see beyond that uniform of yours. The big, strong cop." Quinton grinned and met Wyatt's eyes. "I know that deep down inside is that boy who smiles and pretends that everything is perfect even when it isn't just because that's what boys in foster care do to keep their home." He placed his hand right against Wyatt's cheek. "You don't have to do that with me. I'm not going to turn my back on you." He drew Wyatt to him, bringing their lips together, and then held Wyatt tightly, letting their warmth meld.

Callum began to fuss, and Wyatt lifted him out of the carrier. "It seems he doesn't want to be left out."

Quinton smiled and hated to ruin the mood, but he had to know. "What's going to happen to Jennifer? I know it sounds stupid to be worried about her, but she is Callum's mother." He hoped that someday Callum would be able to have some sort of healthy relationship with her. Quinton wasn't sure if that was even possible, but he could hope.

"Well, there's some good news and some bad news," Wyatt said. "Her bail has been revoked, and isn't likely to be reinstated because of what she did. But she is working with us, and suddenly Remington is singing like a canary, afraid of what she might say. Now he's cooperating in exchange for a lighter sentence. As a result, we made another arrest and have shut down that particular pipeline and passed information to the DEA. That's all I can say, other than it isn't likely that your friend Caleb is ever going to see the light of day again."

Quinton's eyes widened on their own. "Caleb? Don't say anything, but damn…. If he was behind all this…." He sighed and wondered how David and Steven were going to react. "I just hope the rest of my friends realize just what they were sheltering in their midst." He really did care for them. Daniel and Steven had been his backup for a long time.

"You never know. I'd say to call them in a few days. Nothing will be made public immediately, other than the arrest. We're working to keep this quiet, and I trust you to not say anything." Wyatt seemed worn out, with lines around his eyes and mouth.

"Of course."

"But I can tell you this. No court is going to give Jennifer custody of any child. We'll wait the six months and see where we stand, but I'd say it's likely that you could petition for termination of her parental rights altogether. She's going to spend time in jail for her multiple offenses." Wyatt was so sure.

Quinton knew that the wheels of justice tended to grind forward slowly sometimes. But he had the next six months with Callum.

"So where do we go from here?" Quinton asked.

Wyatt grinned. "I know it's going to sound corny, but forward. We'll figure out what the future brings together."

Callum closed his eyes and settled to sleep in the crook of Wyatt's arm. Quinton stood next to him, Wyatt's other arm around his waist. He could see snapshots of their future, the next week or month, even six months, but after that, everything was wide open... except for Wyatt. He was in all the pictures, and as much as hoping scared Quinton, it was also exciting that together they could be a real family.

# Epilogue

Wyatt stood in the kitchen of his house, the scents of Thanksgiving wrapping around him. His mom had put herself in charge of the food, with Quinton helping. His dad had taken possession of the living room and periodically yelled at the television over whatever game happened to be on. Callum sat in his high chair, watching the proceedings and playing with the baby snacks that Quinton had placed on the tray. Mostly he pushed them around, but occasionally one made it into his mouth.

"Wyatt, dear," his mom started, and he braced for whatever she was going to say next. "I know that you and Quinton have decided to live together. But what I want to know is when you plan to make an honest man out of him." She cocked her elegant eyebrows, and Quinton placed his hand over his mouth to try to hide his laughter… and failed.

"How about you let Quinton and me worry about that? He just started moving his things in." He knew she was kidding, but he had been thinking the same sort of thing. The two of them had decided some time ago to take things one step at a time. The permanent custody hearing for Callum had taken place last week. Jennifer had been there, and Wyatt had to say that orange was definitely her color. The judge had heard her case as well as the reports of the social workers and awarded permanent custody of Callum to Quinton. She was free to pursue supervised visitation once she was out of jail. Jennifer was in no condition to care for Callum and wouldn't be for at least the next eighteen months to two years.

"You know I'm just kidding." She smiled and then gave Callum a tickle. Wyatt's mom was thrilled with Callum and already loved him to death. Not that Wyatt could blame her for a second. As for the baby's father, just looking at Quinton made his heart race a little faster, and the thought of having him in his bed every night... well, that was a delight he couldn't even try to put words to. Not that he and Quinton hadn't spent most of their time together at one place or the other. He stood next to Quinton and slid an arm around his waist. It wasn't official yet, and he didn't want to push, but Wyatt already had Quinton's Christmas present in a small box at the bottom of his sock drawer.

"When do you have to go to work?" Quinton asked.

"My half shift starts at two," he said softly. "I know it sucks. But I'm helping one of the other guys out so he can have a chance at dinner with his family too." He kissed Quinton gently, and Callum squealed happily, banging his tray. "I checked my email this morning, and I'm scheduled to take the detective exam next month. If I pass, I'll be promoted." That earned him another kiss and another squeal from Callum. He had a lot of studying to do, but he fully intended to make the most of this opportunity.

"Dinner will be ready in half an hour," his mom pronounced, and he moved away from Quinton so they could finish the last of the cooking.

"Da," Callum called as Quinton turned away. "Da."

"Yes," Quinton said. "Your first Thanksgiving dinner will be in a few minutes, and I got you some turkey and sweet potatoes with apples for dessert."

"Da!" he said even louder, and Quinton made faces that had him laughing. Wyatt joined him, and Callum wriggled in his chair. Quinton turned to help Wyatt's mother, and Callum looked at Wyatt with those big blue eyes. "Pa…. Pa!"

Wyatt reached for him and lifted Callum out of his chair. "Are you calling me Papa?" he asked, whirling Callum around the room, grinning like an idiot as Callum giggled.

"Pa," Callum said again, and Wyatt hugged him.

"Isn't that sweet?" his mom said quietly, a slight hitch in her voice.

Quinton stood next to Wyatt, and Callum reached for him. "Da…." Then he reached for Wyatt. "Pa…."

"Did you teach him that?" Wyatt asked Quinton, who looked sheepish, and Wyatt had his answer.

"Well, I thought I could be Daddy, you could be Papa, and then we could be a family." All Wyatt could do was nod and pull Quinton to him. He had no words, and he didn't need them. It seemed that Callum had already said it all.

Keep reading for a sneak peek at
*Fire and Glass*
by Andrew Grey,
the next book in the Carlisle Troopers series!

# CHAPTER 1

STATE TROOPER Casey Bombaro got into his patrol car to start his workday and grumbled as he read his messages. He already had two break-in reports to investigate. Now he had a message to come into the office outside Carlisle to pick something up. Well, at least one of the reported break-ins was between his current location and town, so it wouldn't be a wasted trip. He responded to the message and quickly scanned the others before buckling up.

One of the things he loved about being a state trooper was that his car was his office. He didn't sit at a desk pushing paper all day. He was out in the trenches, the primary law enforcement presence for a good part of his district, and Casey liked it when the area under his patrol was quiet. It hadn't been for the past few months, and Casey had a pretty good idea what had changed, but he wasn't making progress getting to the source, which frustrated him no end.

He started the engine, pulled out of his driveway, and used GPS to guide him to the address of the break-in. This one was typical of what he'd been finding—the owners came home from a night out to find their home had been broken into. Easily sold electronics were gone, and so was the liquor. Medicine cabinet stripped of prescription meds, and any available jewelry cases or boxes were missing. Nothing else was touched and no messes were made. In each case, the thieves seemed to know what they were looking for and got in and out, leaving very little trace of themselves. The fuckers knew what they were doing, and that was what ground at Casey. The jobs were small-time enough—no big scores up to this point—but it kept happening, sometimes three or four a week.

After making notes about break-in, for which he unfortunately could offer little hope of recovery, he added the report to his list of things to do and headed to the station.

"We got a big job for you," Collins, the sergeant in charge, said with an evil smile even as he handed Casey a cup of coffee. Then he set a small, battered fabric purse on his desk. "This was found behind a business in Newville. It was turned over to the township, and they passed it on to us to try to return. There was ID inside, so sometime today, could you stop by the house and try to return it to the owner?"

Casey grumbled. "Is that why I had to come in?"

Collins narrowed his gaze. "Don't be a growly pain in the ass. I even gave you coffee. I know it's inconvenient, but it's something we can do to help people. Remember? That's part of our job. Just like we're supposed to be a team." He leaned forward, lowering his voice. "You're a good trooper and you take the job seriously as a heart attack, but your people skills suck. None of the others want to work with you because every fucking thing is a competition. Well, knock it off. This isn't some sort of contest to see who can have the quietest patrol district. I will tell you, you could be up for an award: asshole of the year. Whatever stick got lodged up your backside, you need to get rid of it."

"I do my job and I do it well," Casey knew that. He took pride in doing the best job he could. He lived for the job. Hell, it was almost all he had.

"Yeah, you're so good that other troopers stay away. Just cut the arrogance down a notch and work on getting along with your fellow troopers, because I sure as hell don't want to be writing you up for this." His gaze was rock hard, and Casey swallowed. "You've been up for promotion, and it isn't going to happen until you are able to work better with others. It's that simple." His expression softened a little. "I know you want this, and you're a good trooper, but dammit, if others won't work with you, how can you lead them?" The sergeant straightened up. "Go on and get back out there."

Casey took the coffee and headed back to his car, making an effort to say good morning to others as he passed.

"What's with the purse? Trying out a new look?" Wyatt Nelson asked as he passed.

Casey's first instinct was to snark at him, but he swallowed it. "Just some lost property to return."

Wyatt paused in his steps. "Of course. That most definitely isn't your color, and it doesn't go with your shoes at all." He smiled and rolled his eyes. "Come on, Casey. I was only kidding. What's under your skin?"

"It's nothing," he said gently. "Just more work than I have hours. You know how it is." Their districts were next to each other and sometimes overlapped, given the area.

"Yeah, I do. If you need backup, let me know."

"I can…." He stopped himself. His first instinct was to say he could handle things in his district just fine, as though Wyatt had been taking a dig at him. But Wyatt's open expression stopped him. "Thanks. I appreciate the offer. You do the same." He lifted the bag in his hand. "Okay, I need to return my fashion accessory to its rightful owner." A smile crossed his lips. "I'll see you later."

Wyatt half jogged into the building, and Casey got in his patrol car. He had another break-in to investigate and the purse to return, and that was before any more reports came in, which was a certainty given the way things had been going lately. He just wished he could get a handle on these break-ins. Casey knew they were related, but other than MO, there was very little to go on.

HIS FIRST stop was another robbery investigation. The story was much the same. The owners were gone for the evening, and when they returned, their house had been broken into. The same types of items had been stolen. So far Casey had nine incidents in the past four weeks. He took down the details and made notes of the similarities to the others, leaving behind yet another set of shaken and frightened homeowners who wanted the same answers that Casey did.

Back in his patrol car, he took a few minutes to review his notes before heading to the address on the identification in the purse. The drive took about ten minutes before he pulled onto the gravel two-track that led up to the house. He slowly got out of the car and took in his surroundings. There were no cars and no sound. Casey wasn't sure anyone was home until the curtains on the nearest window moved to the side and then slid back into place.

His boots crunched on the gravel, and birds sang in the nearby trees while cicadas hummed their mating song as he went up to the front door. He knocked firmly, carrying the purse under his arm. Casey knocked again when he didn't get an answer, knowing someone was inside. Soft footsteps behind the door told him someone was indeed home, and he was about to knock again when he heard locks disengaging and then the door cracked open a couple of inches. A kid peered through the crack.

"Is your mother home?" Casey asked and didn't get an answer. "I'm with the police, and I have her purse. Can you get her, please?" The chain was still on the door. It closed, and then, after some fumbling and clinking, opened again.

"Mommy isn't home," a little boy about ten years old said.

"Is your dad here?" Casey asked, becoming concerned when the boy shrugged. "Who's home with you?"

"Mama will be back," the boy said, his voice high and pitched with fear and worry.

"It's okay. I have her purse. Is it okay if I bring it inside? I'm a policeman." He knelt down. "You know that the police are here to help you, right?" He had taught Stranger Danger classes and knew he needed to be careful. He didn't want to scare the kid, but he wondered what was really going on. While he waited, one more face peered out from behind the boy, a little girl Casey guessed might be five or six, holding a stuffed rabbit.

"Mama says not to talk to strangers, and I'm not supposed to let anyone in the house." The little boy was scared; that was obvious. But there was something more to it than that.

"Let me bring in your mama's purse. I'm not going to hurt you." God, he hoped he sounded as kind and gentle as he was trying to. "Are you two home alone?"

The boy shook his head. "Beau is here too."

Casey breathed a little easier. "How old is he?" He hoped Beau was the babysitter.

"Four," the little boy answered, and it dawned on Casey that there were three little kids without an adult.

"How long has your mommy been gone?" Casey asked.

The little girl began to cry. "I want Mommy," she whimpered, and the boy lowered his head.

Casey knelt down but didn't make any move to go inside. "When did you see your mama last?" The boy shrugged. "Was it today?" Casey half whispered in an effort to be gentle. The boy shook his head. "Yesterday?" Another head shake. "It's okay. I'm going to help you, I promise." Fuck, he had seen a hell of a lot of shit that people did to one another. A killing that gave him nightmares for weeks, men hitting their wives and girlfriends. Those calls got to him every time. He'd seen the worst kind of hurt, but these three kids—and he hoped there weren't more—touched his heart. And after six years on the job, Casey had come to wonder if that was even possible any longer. It was just easier to wall it off than to let it get battered day in and day out.

"What's your name?" Casey asked, deciding to take things really slow. "I'm Trooper Casey."

"Phillip," the boy answered softly.

He leaned a little closer. "And what's your name?" he asked the little girl.

"That's Jolie," Phillip answered as Jolie slunk behind him.

He wasn't going to push inside. "Have you had enough to eat?"

"I'm hungry," Jolie whispered and started crying again.

"It's okay. Do you want my help to get something to eat?" Casey asked, holding out his hand. Phillip stared at it and then took it.

Relief washed over Casey as he slowly got up and followed Phillip into the house. It was pretty clean. The house seemed to have been vacuumed and dusted. He did a quick sweep of the house and checked upstairs before returning.

"What have you been eating?" Casey asked as he went in through the living and dining areas to the kitchen. A pile of dishes sat in the sink, mostly plates and cups.

"Peanut butter and jelly," Jolie answered as Casey opened the refrigerator. It held very little. Some condiments, a nearly empty jar of jam, a quarter of a jar of peanut butter, some pickles, and a half-empty jug of milk. The cupboards weren't much fuller, with a few boxes of macaroni and cheese and some spices. He didn't see any bread or even crackers. God, these kids were down to the very end of their food.

"Where's Beau?" Casey asked Phillip.

"Hiding," Phillip answered.

"Why don't you both go find him, and I'll make you some macaroni and cheese. Okay?" God, there were so many things running through his head, but he didn't want to panic the kids. They were already under enough stress. Once they hurried away, he called in and requested Wyatt's backup, got some water on the stove to get the kids fed, and then made a call to Child Services.

The kids returned, littlest one in tow. Little Beau was adorable, with a head of unruly brown hair, huge brown eyes, and his thumb stuck firmly in his mouth. "Are you Beau?" Casey asked gently, and Beau nodded,

leaving his thumb firmly in place. "Do you like macaroni and cheese?" He nodded again, holding Phillip's
hand. "Good. Jolie said she was hungry, so I wanted to
make you something to eat."

"No peanut butter?" Jolie asked, and when Casey
shook his head, she grinned. "Good."

Once he got the boxed mac and cheese finished,
Phillip got out what seemed to be the last of the clean
dishes in the cupboard and the last clean silverware
in the drawer. Once again Casey wondered how long
these poor children had been in the house all alone.
Once he got the food dished up and Phillip got them the
last of the milk, Casey stepped out of the room to call
the sergeant.

"What's going on?" the sergeant asked urgently.

"That purse you gave me to return has opened a
whole kettle of worms. I got here, and the lady it be-
longs to is nowhere to be found. Her three children are
at the house alone, probably have been for days." He
wanted to be sick at the thought. What kind of parent
did this sort of thing? "I needed you to know that this is
going to take a while. I don't think they've eaten much,
so I made them something to eat. Wyatt is going to be
over soon, and I called Child Services."

"Good. Keep the kids calm and find out what you
can from them. Maybe we can find a relative in the area
who will take them. Call in names, and I'll have people
here get on it."

"Okay," Casey agreed, still a little nervous about
providing unexpected child care. "All three of them are
eating like they haven't had a hot meal in days."

"And idea how long they've been alone?"

"Guessing five days to a week. The poor things
have eaten what they can and are nearly out of food."

He spoke softly, looking out the window to see Wyatt pull up in his patrol car, followed by a dark sedan that he hoped was Child Services. "I'll send you any information I can get." They ended the call, and Casey let Wyatt and Donald Ickle inside. Then he returned to the kitchen to find Phillip and Jolie at the table, but Beau missing.

"Where is he?"

"Hiding," Jolie said. "Strange men scare him. There were people in the garage a few days ago, and it scared him really bad."

"Will you check that out?" Casey asked Wyatt. He easily found Beau hiding in one of the cupboards. He gently bent down, talking softly and holding out his hand. Once Beau took it, he lifted the little boy, hugging him, surprised when Beau put his arms around his neck and held tightly enough to nearly cut off his air. "Are you still hungry?" Casey asked, rubbing his back.

"Want Mama," he cried.

"I know. I'm going to try to find her for you." What the hell else was he supposed to say? "I promise. Do you want to eat some more?"

"Sit with me," Phillip said, and Beau went to his brother and sat on his lap. Casey pushed the plate over to him and swallowed hard. Then he tilted his head toward the other room, and Donald followed him.

"What have we got here?" Donald asked with a sigh.

"Mom missing for nearly a week, I'd guess. Father not around. I made them something to eat because they looked half-starved and there was little food in the house. Ummm...." He cleared his throat.

"It's okay. If these sorts of things don't get to you, then you aren't human. And believe me, I've seen worse. At least these three are fed and relatively clean. And they seem to trust you to a degree. Introduce me as Donny and tell them that I'm going to help them find their mother too."

"I'm hoping we can locate a relative that will take them," Casey said, and Donald nodded.

Casey returned to the kitchen and introduced Donald.

"Phillip, do you have an aunt or an uncle that you see?" Casey asked Phillip, hoping he would know the most information. But he shook his head. "Is there anyone you know? A cousin? Maybe a close friend of your mom's?" The kids all look at one another blankly. "What about your grandma and grandpa?" Another shake of the head. "Do you have any relatives close by?" He was becoming a little desperate.

"There's Uncle Bert, but Mama says he doesn't like us. Mama had a fight with him, so we don't see him anymore."

"Mama says he's mean and doesn't care," Jolie supplied.

"Is your Uncle Bert's last name Riley too?" he asked, and Phillip shrugged. Casey wrote it down anyway, wondering why the name sounded familiar, and had to hope for the best. He messaged the sergeant with the information, along with the kids' names and ages. Maybe there were records that would help. Anything so these kids could be properly taken care of.

"You did really good," Donald told Phillip, who finished up his food and put his dishes in the nearly overflowing sink. He then helped the littler ones before they wandered off into the living room, sat on the sofa, and turned on the television.

"What the…?" Casey asked Donald.

"They're fed and calm, and that's the best thing for now. Let's hope that we can find a relative who will take them. But if not, I'll make some calls."

Wyatt came inside, his expression grim. "Someone was in the garage, and it's my guess that they took whatever had any value at all. The place was pretty well cleaned out, but I have no idea what they might have gotten without the owner to tell us. I doubt the kids would know, but there was definite evidence of a break-in."

"Any sign of who might have done it? Other than things missing."

Wyatt shrugged. "I don't know. It's like stuff isn't there any longer, but that's about all. It looked like the side door was just open and they got in easily."

"But they made noise, and that scared the kids," Casey said. "Who may have seen something. I'm pretty sure little Beau hid, but the others might have looked outside."

"I'll ask them," Wyatt offered, but Casey put his hand on his arm, stopping him.

"No," he said gently.

"Casey's right. It should be him," Donald said and went in to the living room.

Casey paused and decided that he didn't need to ask those questions at that moment. Beau sat on Phillip's lap, the older boy's arms cradling his brother. Jolie sat next to both of them, hugging the stuffed rabbit, leaning on Phillip, all three of them comforting each other. The last thing he wanted to do was add more stress with his questions.

His phone vibrated, and Casey left them alone to take the call in the kitchen, away from the kids. "Hey, Sarge."

"We located a relative, the uncle. His name is Bertram Riley, and he lives on East South Street in Carlisle. I'll text you the address and phone number. I suggest contacting him. See what he's willing to do."

"I will. Thank you," he said and then punched in the numbers from the text. He would prefer to do this in person, but showing up at the guy's front door might be more of a shock.

"Mr. Riley?" he asked once the call connected.

"Yes…"

"I'm Trooper Casey Bombaro with the state police. Do you know Phillip, Beau, and Jolie?" he asked, hoping to trigger something.

"Yes. They're my sister's children. Has something happened to them? Has Janet done something?" The second question was asked as though he expected a positive answer. Then the tone changed "Case, what's happened?"

That nickname and the voice triggered an old, strong memory. Something—someone—he hadn't thought about in years.

"Bertie?" he asked softly. He probably should have put the pieces together before this, but the thought had never occurred to him. And just like that, memories flooded back. The two of them in class, the way Bertie couldn't seem to take his gaze off him. The lunches they had together with their group of friends. Casey pulled his attention out of the past, back where it belonged. "The kids are okay," he said. "But we can't locate Janet, and it looks like she could have been gone for as long as a week."

A sharp gasp reached through the phone, followed by a near panic. "I'll be right there." Now it was Casey's turn to feel as though the ground had shifted under his feet as his heart beat just a little faster, knowing he was going to see the first guy he'd fallen in love with. Casey chided himself that he needed to get his head in the game and not on some flight of fancy. But still, he couldn't stop the jolt of excitement that lingered for longer than it should.

ANDREW GREY is the author of more than one hundred works of Contemporary Gay Romantic fiction. After twenty-seven years in corporate America, he has now settled down in Central Pennsylvania with his husband of more than twenty-five years, Dominic, and his laptop. An interesting ménage. Andrew grew up in western Michigan with a father who loved to tell stories and a mother who loved to read them. Since then he has lived throughout the country and traveled throughout the world. He is a recipient of the RWA Centennial Award, has a master's degree from the University of Wisconsin–Milwaukee, and now writes full-time. Andrew's hobbies include collecting antiques, gardening, and leaving his dirty dishes anywhere but in the sink (particularly when writing). He considers himself blessed with an accepting family, fantastic friends, and the world's most supportive and loving partner. Andrew currently lives in beautiful, historic Carlisle, Pennsylvania.

Email:andrewgrey@comcast.net

Website: www.andrewgreybooks.com

# FIRE AND WATER

## ANDREW GREY

CARLISLE COPS

1

A Carlisle Cops Novel

Officer Red Markham knows about the ugly side of life after a car accident left him scarred and his parents dead. His job policing the streets of Carlisle, PA, only adds to the ugliness, and lately, drug overdoses have been on the rise. One afternoon, Red is dispatched to the local Y for a drowning accident involving a child. Arriving on site, he finds the boy rescued by lifeguard Terry Baumgartner. Of course, Red isn't surprised when gorgeous Terry won't give him and his ugly mug the time of day.

Overhearing one of the officer's comments about him being shallow opens Terry's eyes. Maybe he isn't as kindhearted as he always thought. His friend Julie suggests he help those less fortunate by delivering food to the elderly. On his route he meets outspoken Margie, a woman who says what's on her mind. Turns out, she's Officer Red's aunt.

Red and Terry's worlds collide as Red tries to track the source of the drugs and protect Terry from an ex-boyfriend who won't take no for an answer. Together they might discover a chance for more than they expected—if they can see beyond what's on the surface.

# www.dreamspinnerpress.com

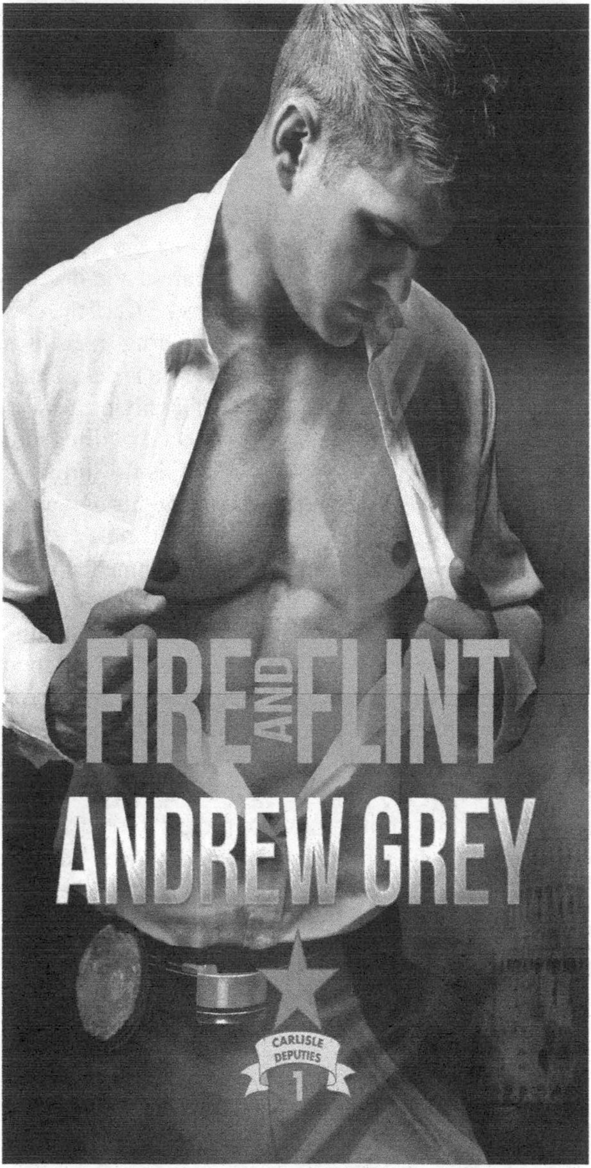
FIRE AND FLINT
ANDREW GREY
CARLISLE DEPUTIES
1

A Carlisle Deputies Novel

Jordan Erichsohn suspects something is rotten about his boss, Judge Crawford. Unfortunately he has nowhere to turn and doubts anyone will believe his claims—least of all the handsome deputy, Pierre Ravelle, who has been assigned to protect the judge after he received threatening letters. The judge has a long reach, and if he finds out Jordan's turned on him, he might impede Jordan adopting his son, Jeremiah.

When Jordan can no longer stay silent, he gathers his courage and tells Pierre what he knows. To his surprise and relief, Pierre believes him, and Jordan finds an ally… and maybe more. Pierre vows to do what it takes to protect Jordan and Jeremiah and see justice done. He's willing to fight for the man he's growing to love and the family he's starting to think of as his own. But Crawford is a powerful and dangerous enemy, and he's not above ripping apart everything Jordan and Pierre are trying to build in order to save himself….

# www.dreamspinnerpress.com

# REDEMPTION
## BY FIRE

ANDREW GREY

By Fire Series: Book One

Dirk Krause is an asshole of the first degree. His life is a hell of his own making, and he makes everyone around him just as miserable. When he's injured on the job while fighting a fire, he's nearly unbearable to the hospital staff, and of course no one from his unit cares enough to visit.

Lee Stockton is the new guy at the station, so he gets saddled with the job of bringing Dirk a sympathy bouquet from the guys at the firehouse. To Dirk's surprise, Lee sees through him like a pane of glass and doesn't take any of his crap. Lee's determined to get Dirk to stop being a dick just to push everyone away. When their fighting turns to fucking, will the fireworks shine brightly on a possible relationship or leave them with nothing but ashes?

# www.dreamspinnerpress.com

# REKINDLED FLAME

# ANDREW GREY

Rekindled Flame: Book One

Firefighter Morgan has worked hard to build a home for himself after a nomadic childhood. When Morgan is called to a fire, he finds the family out front, but their tenant still inside. He rescues Richard Smalley, who turns out to be an old friend he hasn't seen in years and the one person he regretted leaving behind.

Richard has had a hard life. He served in the military, where he lost the use of his legs, and has been struggling to make his way since coming home. Now that he no longer has a place to live, Morgan takes him in, but when someone attempts to set fire to Morgan's house, they both become suspicious and wonder what's going on.

Years ago Morgan was gutted when he moved away, leaving Richard behind, so he's happy to pick things up where they left off. But now that Richard seems to be the target of an arsonist, he may not be the safest person to be around.

# www.dreamspinnerpress.com

# BAD
## TO BE GOOD

ANDREW GREY

Bad to Be Good: Book One

Longboat Key, Florida, is about as far from the streets of Detroit as a group of gay former mobsters can get, but threats from within their own organization forced them into witness protection—and a new life.

Richard Marsden is making the best of his second chance, tending bar and learning who he is outside of organized crime… and flirting with the cute single dad, Daniel, who comes in every Wednesday. But much like Richard, Daniel hides dark secrets that could get him killed. When Daniel's past as a hacker catches up to him, Richard has the skills to help Daniel out, but not without raising some serious questions and risking his own new identity and the friends who went into hiding with him.

Solving problems like Daniel's is what Richard does best—and what he's trying to escape. But finding a way to keep Daniel and his son safe without sacrificing the person he's becoming will take some imagination, and the stakes have never been higher. This time it's not just lives on the line—it's his heart….

# www.dreamspinnerpress.com